Will grinned, then went to stand up as Jake, who'd tackled him first, began to drag himself to an upright position. But Will's right leg was awkwardly positioned under Jake's forearm, and as Jake released himself, Will felt his knee try to follow, twisting hard in the wrong direction. Will winced as pain shot through his leg.

"You okay, man?" Josh asked, reaching his hand out to Will. Will took it and let Josh pull him the rest of the way up, feeling his knee continue to burn as he stood. Will felt a flash of worry that he'd injured himself and wouldn't be able to play tonight, but after a couple of seconds the pain faded and his leg felt fine.

"Hey," Josh suggested, brushing dirt off his blue-and-gray-striped shirt, "after we kick some Ridgefield butt, why don't we go out and celebrate you going to Michigan?"

"Sounds good," Will said, casting a backward glance at his dad, who was busy clipping branches. He didn't seem to be paying attention to Will and his friends.

Or maybe he realized that I do deserve a break, Will thought, hoping it was true. His friends knew what a big deal his football career was—and soon enough his dad would understand that football was all Will needed.

Don't miss any of the books in SWEET VALLEY HIGH
SENIOR YEAR, an exciting series from Bantam Books!

Visit the Official Sweet Valley Web Site on the Internet at:

http://www.sweetvalley.com

Francine Pascal's SVH senior year

Nothing Is Forever

CREATED BY
FRANCINE PASCAL

BANTAM BOOKS
NEW YORK · TORONTO · LONDON · SYDNEY · AUCKLAND

RL: 6, AGES 012 AND UP

NOTHING IS FOREVER
A Bantam Book / August 2000

Sweet Valley High® is a registered trademark of Francine Pascal.
Conceived by Francine Pascal.
Cover photography by Michael Segal.

Produced by 17th Street Productions,
an Alloy Online, Inc. company.
33 West 17th Street
New York, NY 10011.

ISBN: 0-553-49336-1

Visit us on the Web! www.randomhouse.com/teens

Published simultaneously in the United States and Canada

Bantam Books is an imprint of Random House Children's Books, a
division of Random House, Inc. BANTAM BOOKS and the rooster
colophon are registered trademarks of Random House, Inc. Bantam Books,
1540 Broadway, New York, New York 10036.

PRINTED IN THE UNITED STATES OF AMERICA

OPM   0 9 8 7 6 5 4 3 2 1

To Kacey Michelle Cotton

Ken Matthews

One of my first real memories is of football.

I guess I was around three, and my dad was watching the Super Bowl. I'd just woken up from a nap, and I found him in front of the TV. He pulled me into his lap and said, "Watch this, Ken. That man is gonna throw the ball all the way to the other end of the field!"

I could tell from the way my dad said it that he thought that was pretty much the most amazing thing a person could do.

So I watched. And the guy did it. And it really did look amazing.

"Who is that man?" I asked.

My dad laughed. "He's the quarter-back," he explained.

"I'm going to be a quarterback, Dad," I told him.

He laughed again and ruffled my hair.

melissa Fox

<u>Reasons</u> <u>to</u> <u>go</u> <u>to</u> <u>michigan</u>:

1. Will
2. Great cheerleading squad
3. Will
4. Solid liberal-arts program
5. Way too far away for my mother to show up for any surprise visits
6. Will
7. I look great in blue and gold.
8. Will
9. Will
10. Will

Jessica Wakefield

Jade. That's a stone, isn't it? Like, stone-cold?

I still can't believe she actually cheated on Jeremy. Doesn't the word <u>loyalty</u> mean anything to her? What about self-control?

But if she wants to go around acting like that, fine. What Jade Wu does with her reputation is her problem. The only reason I care at all is because of Jeremy. How could she hurt someone as incredible as him just because she couldn't keep her hands off another guy? Anyone who would do that deserves . . .

Okay — so does the word <u>hypocrite</u> mean anything to me?

Maybe I should just stay out of it.

Maybe.

Jeremy Aames

I always heard that girls were the ones who wanted commitment, relationships, all that stuff. Guys are supposed to be these total jerks who just use girls or cheat on them.

You really shouldn't believe what you hear.

Andy Marsden

A lot's been going on with everybody lately. I realize that. But I've gotta admit—I sort of figured that announcing to my friends that I'm gay would have <u>some</u> kind of effect. Tia, Liz, Jessica, Maria . . . it's not like any of them usually misses a chance for drama. But somehow brooding boy still manages to keep them all too busy to remember anything—or anyone—else.

I thought this was one of those things that you go to your female friends with. Girls are supposed to be better listeners, right? But I guess I went about this all wrong. Maybe I should try brooding boy himself—Conner McDermott.

CHAPTER
Absolute Perfection
1

Will Simmons woke up on Saturday morning to broad beams of sunshine streaming through his blinds. He blinked and stretched his muscular arms out above his head. This was exactly how today should begin. The day Hank Krubowski, the University of Michigan scout, was taking the entire Simmons family—along with Will's girlfriend, Melissa—to breakfast to officially welcome Will to the great Michigan football organization.

Will sat up slowly and rolled his head around on his shoulders. He ran a hand through his blond hair, smoothing down the few strands that always stood straight up first thing in the morning.

Glancing across the room to his dresser, Will's eyes landed on the gold frame that stood right in the center. He focused on Melissa's gleaming smile and piercing blue eyes, remembering the day he'd taken that shot. It was their anniversary last year, and she'd been so happy, she practically *glowed*.

We had no idea what we were in for this year, Will thought, shaking his head. He stood, then turned to straighten his dark blue cotton sheets, pulling them neatly up to his pillows. He and Melissa had faced some rough times, but the experience had only brought them closer. He knew for sure now that he belonged with her, and luckily she was equally convinced. Even though Michigan wasn't really her first choice, she was just as psyched to go there as he was—because all that mattered to her was that they were together.

His life was as close to perfection as possible, Will decided as he grabbed a pair of gray running shorts from his dresser drawer. He had his scholarship, he had Melissa, and tonight he would be leading Sweet Valley to another victory by destroying Ridgefield High.

Quickly throwing on an old El Carro T-shirt and some socks and sneakers, Will headed out into the hall. He was planning on squeezing in a quick run before he had to shower and get ready for brunch. Halfway down the stairs, Will heard the phone ring. He paused, waiting to hear if someone else answered it.

"Will, it's Melissa," his mom called out from the kitchen.

Will grinned, then hurried down the rest of the stairs and into the kitchen, where his mom stood by the kitchen counter, holding the black cordless phone out to him.

"Thanks, Mom," he said, then took the phone

from her and strolled into the family room, plopping down on his dad's leather armchair.

He pressed the phone to his ear. "Hi, Liss."

"Hey."

Will could hear the familiar crackling static of a cell-phone connection. "Where are you?" he asked, frowning in concern. She couldn't have forgotten about brunch today—she knew what a big deal this was for him. For *both* of them.

"On my way to the mall, to meet Cherie," she answered.

Will rolled his eyes. Melissa and her friends probably spent more time at the mall than they did sleeping. He glanced over at the tall wooden grandfather clock against the opposite wall. "You didn't forget about—"

"I wouldn't miss brunch for anything," Melissa interrupted smoothly. "I just need to stop and pick up something."

Will's smile returned at the teasing note in her voice. He had a feeling that whatever she was "picking up" had something to do with him.

"It's a surprise," she added with a laugh. "But don't worry—I'll be at your house by eleven."

"Great," Will said, jumping up. "See ya then."

He clicked off the phone and placed it facedown on the glass coffee table in front of him.

"I'm going for a run," he called to his mom. "I'll be back soon. Make sure Dad gets up."

The second he stepped outside, Will blinked at

3

the bright sunshine, enjoying the warm rays hitting his bare arms and legs. He took off at a jog, slowly increasing his speed as he ran. His muscles responded, loosening with every step, and his running form was even more clean, more flawless than usual.

It was pretty incredible, Will reflected as he felt himself settle into an easy rhythm. Like all the forces of nature or fate or something were working together to make his life absolutely perfect. At this rate Will could probably run all the way to Michigan without breaking a sweat.

Melissa Fox held the oversized navy sweatshirt up in front of her, narrowing her blue eyes at the enormous block-letter *M* stitched in yellow-gold on the front.

"What do you think?" she asked Cherie Reese, biting her lip.

Cherie lifted her small shoulders in a shrug. The expression in her light eyes was beyond bored. "It's huge," she observed blandly.

"Right," Melissa said, flicking away a piece of blue thread that was hanging down from the sleeve. "It has to be. Will's got very broad shoulders."

They were in a store called The Fan Club, filled with hats, jackets, sweatshirts, and other clothing items all emblazoned with the logos of nearly every professional and collegiate sports team in America.

Melissa had gotten the idea to come here when

4

she saw her dad wearing his old Colgate University T-shirt this morning. She wanted this day to be perfect for Will—they were finally living their dream, and she planned on enjoying every second of it.

Melissa gazed at the shirt, running a perfectly polished fingernail along the chunky gold *M*. "He's going to look great in this," she said. "Then again, Will looks great in everything," she added.

"Excuse me while I hurl," Cherie said, rolling her eyes.

Melissa laughed. "I'm just proud of him," she said, folding the sweatshirt over her arm. She started to stroll toward the back of the store, Cherie following her. "I think he needs to show off a little—let the whole world know where he's going."

"I think the whole world already knows," Cherie teased. "You've been bragging about it enough."

"Have I mentioned that he's going on a *full* scholarship?" Melissa asked, catching sight of a rack of smaller sweatshirts in the corner under a sign saying Women's.

"Only like four hundred and eighty-five times," Cherie muttered.

Melissa flashed her friend a quick smile, then hurried over to the rack. She pushed aside the mediums until she reached the small section, then pulled out a formfitting sweatshirt with the words *University of Michigan* in script across the front. Holding it up against her chest to check the fit,

Melissa silently noted that the deep blue material would look great with her pale eyes.

Cherie groaned. "If you two are going to start dressing alike, I swear, I really *will* hurl."

Melissa ignored the comment and laid the smaller sweatshirt on her arm, over the large one she'd chosen for Will.

Cherie sighed. "Don't you want to wait and get a sweatshirt for the college *you're* going to?" she persisted.

Melissa glanced at Cherie, raising her eyebrows. "That's what I'm doing," she explained.

Cherie blinked. "What?"

"Michigan *is* my school." Melissa was unable to keep the tiny note of excitement out of her voice. She spun around and started heading back up front to the register, smiling to herself.

"Since when?" Cherie asked, striding after Melissa. "You haven't even applied yet."

Melissa waited to answer until she and Cherie had stepped into line, right behind a scruffy-looking kid and his big, burly father. The two of them were loaded down with Los Angeles Lakers hats and clothes.

"Actually," Melissa began, "I sent in my application, and the guidance counselor thinks I've got a great chance. We already know Will's in, so basically . . . it's all set."

Cherie flipped her red curls back behind her shoulder. "Wait a second," she said, moving closer to

Melissa to let someone pass behind her. "I thought you were all into USC."

Melissa shrugged. "I was," she said. "But the more I thought about it, the more I realized that Michigan was really the best place to be."

A twinge of doubt passed through Melissa, gone almost before she could recognize the emotion. Why did Cherie have to make such a big deal out of this? It was *her* choice if she'd rather be with Will.

The people in front of Melissa finished and walked away, so Melissa stepped forward and placed her sweatshirts down on the glass counter, handing her credit card to the muscular salesclerk. He gave his sun-bleached bangs a toss and flashed her a flirty smile, which Melissa didn't bother to return.

"So you're just going to follow Will," Cherie said, picking at the metallic paint chipping on her nails.

Melissa paused while the guy gave her the receipt to sign. She quickly scrawled her name at the bottom, then handed it back to him. "I wouldn't call it *following* him," she replied. After all, there was plenty at Michigan for *her* too.

Cherie gave a little snort. "Well, I would." She rolled her eyes. "Michigan was Will's idea, right? Not yours."

"It was *our* idea," Melissa responded. She practically snatched her credit card back from the guy's outstretched hand, then grabbed the bag containing the sweatshirts and stalked out of the store.

Cherie chased after her. "You two aren't getting married or something, are you?" she asked, her eyes wide with horror.

Melissa pursed her lips, wondering why Cherie wouldn't just drop it. "Why? What if we are?" she asked, glancing at the store windows as they speed walked by them.

"Are you?" Cherie's voice rose in panic. "Melissa . . ."

Melissa laughed. "Relax. We're not getting married." She slung the sweatshirt bag over her shoulder. "Yet."

Cherie stood still, staring at Melissa with wide, shocked eyes. "What's that supposed to mean?" she demanded.

"We've been together forever, and we're going to stay together," Melissa responded. Gazing across the mall, she noticed the bright signs in the food court, and the small rumbling of hunger in her stomach reminded her that she had to get going to be on time for Will's brunch.

"Come on," she urged Cherie, quickening her pace as she started walking again.

Cherie hurried to keep up. "Okay, so you and Will are the real thing," she said. "But—I don't know—do you really think it's a good idea to follow him to college?"

"Will you stop using that word?" Melissa snapped. "It makes me sound like a puppy dog or something. I won't be *following* him. I'll just be *joining* him." But even as she said it, that twinge of anxiety from before returned.

"I guess I just thought you'd be looking forward to having a little freedom," Cherie remarked.

Melissa took a deep breath, ready to explode. Since when did Cherie actually think for herself anyway?

"Look, I really have to go," Melissa said as they reached the mall exit.

"I think I'm gonna stay and check out a few shoe stores," Cherie said. "I need gray platforms to go with that new miniskirt I got last week."

"So I'll see you later." Melissa leaned into the door, opening it a crack. "Let's meet at school when I'm done with brunch, okay?"

"School?" Cherie scrunched her small features together in confusion. "Why?"

"So we can make banners for the game against Ridgefield tonight," Melissa explained, pushing the door farther open with her back. "I want to make a big one for Will. Call Gina and Lila," Melissa added as she headed outside. "And Amy and Renee. Tell them to meet us there at twelve-thirty."

"Okay," Cherie agreed, her perky smile returning. Melissa gave Cherie one last wave good-bye, then turned and hurried out of the mall.

Melissa couldn't help feeling agitated as she scanned the parking lot, unable to recall where she'd parked. Why was she letting Cherie get to her?

Cherie didn't know anything about Melissa and Will's relationship. She didn't get what really mattered to them.

Finally Melissa spotted her mom's Explorer and let out a deep sigh, reminding herself that this was supposed to be her and Will's day, and nothing could ruin that. After all, Melissa and Will had everything they needed: each other.

Jessica swung open the door to House of Java with exactly four seconds to spare before being officially late. She'd purposely stalled this morning, not wanting to spend one moment more in the place than she had to. Last night had been a disaster, and she knew there would be aftershocks this morning. Her brain was still looping the instant replay of the whole awful event. First she saw Jeremy cutting Jade down in front of everyone at Crescent Beach—a good thing—and then she flashed to him turning on Jessica and letting her have it even worse—a bad thing. *Very* bad.

The bell on the door announced her arrival with an inappropriately happy jingle. At least it was only nine-thirty; the place was basically empty since most of HOJ's clients were high-school students who rarely dragged their butts out of bed before eleven on Saturdays.

Bed would be nice, Jessica thought with a yearning sigh as she let the door close behind her and stepped inside the coffeehouse. She was immediately surrounded by the rich smell of coffee, an aroma that was becoming as familiar to her as her mom's kitchen.

Jessica took a deep breath and glanced over at the counter, but no one stood behind it. She scanned the room for her coworkers. Corey and Jade were both scheduled to work with her this morning.

She found Corey sitting near the window, finishing a cigarette. The sun through the blinds flashed off the narrow silver hoop in Corey's nose. Corey narrowed her eyes at Jessica, and they practically disappeared into the kohl-black smudges of eyeliner that rimmed them. Quickly putting out her cigarette, Corey jumped up and grabbed a napkin to wipe down the table next to her, trying very hard to look busy.

There's one perk about being an assistant manager, Jessica thought. She almost smiled. It was fun to have that effect on her coworkers.

"Well, if it isn't Gwyneth Paltrow," a familiar voice snapped from behind Jessica.

Slowly Jessica turned around, feeling her jaw tighten in anticipation of a confrontation.

Jade stood facing her, an angry glare contorting her normally attractive features. Jade was one coworker who wouldn't clean up her act for Jessica even if Jessica owned the place.

"So, Miss Drama Queen," Jade hissed, taking a

11

step toward Jessica. "I'm just curious—what were you expecting to get out of last night's little performance? I think I've got it down, but I just want to be sure. Your main objectives were to humiliate me, crush Jeremy, and make a complete fool out of yourself, right?"

Jessica's shoulders sagged. Hurting Jeremy had been the last thing she'd intended—she'd just wanted to help him.

"Don't start, Jade," Jessica said, attempting to keep her voice firm despite all the emotions whirling around inside her. "I don't want to hear it." She started to walk toward the employee lounge.

"Oh, and I'm supposed to care?" Jade called after Jessica.

Jessica winced, glancing around at the few customers sitting at the mismatched tables and booths. Most of the customers seemed oblivious—but one woman had apparently been watching. She quickly averted her eyes when Jessica looked at her.

Jessica hurried back to the lounge before Jade could say anything else, taking deep breaths to slow down her heartbeat as she opened her locker and pulled out her green apron.

Just as she finished tying the apron around her waist, the door to the lounge swung open and Jade stalked in.

"Why don't you just admit it?" Jade asked, reaching up to push a few strands of straight dark hair

12

back into the loose bun on the back of her head. "You're jealous."

"Right," Jessica replied, letting out a sound somewhere between a snort and a laugh. "I'm jealous of a sneaky, selfish little liar who's too stupid to realize when she's got a great guy like Jeremy." Jessica was pretty sure she saw Jade flinch, and she felt a small spark of triumph.

Jade nodded slowly, then walked over to straighten the magazines lying on the table next to the old maroon couch. "You just proved my point," she stated calmly, flashing Jessica a small smile. She whirled around and walked out of the lounge.

Jessica paused for a second, frowning in confusion. Why did it feel like Jade had just won somehow? She slammed her locker door shut, then followed Jade back out.

Jade was already behind the counter, fixing a cappuccino for a customer. Jessica waited to approach her until Jade had handed the guy his drink.

"What's that supposed to mean?" Jessica asked as she opened up a new box of coffee filters and carefully began stacking them. "What *point* did I prove?"

Jade grinned, and Jessica was pretty sure she would have smacked her if there hadn't been witnesses. "It's obvious," Jade said, squeezing past Jessica to get to the cinnamon shakers. "You really are just jealous—because Jeremy chose me over you."

It was Jessica's turn to flinch. She clenched her fists into tight balls at her sides.

"Jeremy did *not* choose you over me," Jessica blurted out, feeling her face grow hot. She gave her head a slight shake. "I mean, this isn't about that anyway. This has nothing to do with me."

"Admit it," Jade said, cocking her head. She leaned back against the dark green wall and met Jessica's gaze directly. "You want Jeremy back."

Jessica opened her mouth to deny it, but somehow she couldn't get any words to come out. Why did Jade keep saying this about Jessica when Jade was the one who'd messed up?

Finally Jessica started to feel in control of her voice again. "If I wanted him back," she began in a confident tone. "Then . . ." She trailed off as the door jangled open and a big group of sophomore girls from SVH came in, talking and laughing loudly as they walked up to the counter.

Jade gave Jessica one last frustratingly arrogant smile, then stepped up to take the girls' orders.

Jessica fought to keep her cool, but all she wanted was to lunge at Jade and wring the girl's long, perfect neck.

I can't let her get to me, Jessica told herself, angrily shoving the coffee filters away from her. But she had a feeling that wasn't going to be possible today. *This is going to be one long shift.*

14

Evan Plummer

Okay. Heads, I call Liz. Tails, I don't.
Tails.

Wait. Two out of three?

This is stupid. I'm either going to be
mature and do the right thing, or I'm
going to keep my mouth shut and risk
the possibility of my best friend getting
seriously hurt.

He's not going to listen to me. But
Elizabeth . . . he's different with her.
So maybe if she gave him some kind of
ultimatum—like, "It's me or the booze"—
maybe he'd sit up and take notice.

Okay, so heads, I call Liz. And tails . . .
I call Liz.

Maria Slater

From: mslater@swiftnet.com
To: Sweet Valley Tribune.Sports@SVMedia.com

Letter to the Editor:
   It is the opinion of this reader
that your sportswriter is being
unprofessional, not to mention stupid!
His recent coverage of Sweet Valley
football has spotlighted Will Simmons,
describing the QB as though he's some
kind of sports god.
   Doesn't this writer realize that his
own son is a very good quarterback too,
even if Will is getting more game time?
   Doesn't this writer realize that
he's totally devastating his own kid
by making such a big deal over the
fact that he's spent a couple of
games on the bench?
   And don't I realize that if I send
this to the <u>Tribune,</u> Ken will be
totally humiliated and probably never
speak to me again?

<message deleted>

CHAPTER 2

Remember to Breathe

Saturday. Game day.

Ken rolled over and closed his eyes, but the sunlight sliced through his eyelids, forcing him to wake up. Why couldn't it be raining? Pouring, in fact. Coming down in buckets, with gale-force winds. When was monsoon season anyway? Maybe Sweet Valley could catch the tail end of one of those storms.

Ken would settle for just enough of a drizzle to turn the field into mud. Anything to put him out of his misery. Anything to cancel the game.

But no, it was another perfect California Saturday. The game would go off tonight as scheduled. With golden boy Will Simmons rocketing pass after perfect pass.

And Ken Matthews riding the bench.

Ken groaned, tossing off his plaid quilt and sitting up. He swung his legs over the side of the bed, then dropped his head down into his hands, rubbing his temples.

I can't sit here all day, Ken told himself. He sighed

and stood up, crossing over to his window. He blinked as he peered outside at the concrete sidewalk.

Damn, he realized, moving his gaze to the clock on the wall above his desk. Maria was coming over to go running with him—he'd totally blanked on it, but she was supposed to be here in ten minutes.

The frustration and disappointment he'd woken up to began to fade as he quickly threw on his running clothes, picturing the way Maria's long, sleek legs would look in her red shorts and the glow that would appear on her face once they'd worked up to a fast run.

Ken grinned to himself as he jogged down the stairs two at a time. Maria couldn't care less if Ken was the first-string quarterback or the water boy. He really had no right to sit there feeling sorry for himself when he had someone like her in his life.

Strolling into the kitchen, Ken wrinkled his nose at the smell that greeted him. He noticed the empty box of pepperoni pizza from last night sitting on the counter. He grabbed it and stuffed it into the already overflowing trash can next to the sink. Then he walked over to the windows and pushed them open, hoping the fresh air would get rid of the stale-pizza smell.

I guess that's what happens when two guys live alone, Ken thought as he opened the refrigerator and started searching the top shelf. For a while his dad had actually been taking better care of the house.

When Mr. Matthews was dating Asha, in fact, it had almost been like when Ken's mom was still around, before she moved to Florida.

But Asha's history, Ken reminded himself, finally locating the orange juice behind a couple of beer bottles. His dad had taken care of that when he cheated on her. Ken shook his head and started chugging back the juice directly from the carton. When he finished, he stuck it back in the fridge, then headed out into the hall.

He was on his way to the front door to wait for Maria outside when he heard his dad's voice coming from the den. He couldn't make out what his dad was saying, but it sounded like he was upset. Ken crept quietly down the hall, stopping just outside the doorway to the den. His father had his back to Ken. One hand was clutching the phone to his ear; the other was gripping the edge of his large, oak desk.

"I already told you, Bill," Mr. Matthews said. "I don't want to do it. I have my reasons."

Ken shifted his weight, wondering what this was about. Bill was his dad's editor at the newspaper—it wasn't normal for him to stand up to his boss like that.

"Why don't you let Joe Caruso cover the Sweet Valley game?" Ken's dad continued after a brief pause.

Ken sucked in his breath, folding in on himself as if he'd just been socked by an opposing team's linebacker.

His dad was trying to get out of showing up at *his* game. He was really *that* ashamed of Ken.

"I know, I know," Mr. Matthews said. "But things are different now."

Suddenly the sound of the doorbell ringing reverberated through the house, jolting Ken. Apparently the sound surprised his father too because he jumped and whirled around—facing his son.

Ken didn't have time to mask his hurt expression. Mr. Matthews froze, and his hand seemed to grip the phone hard enough to crush it. Ken stared back at his father, searching his face for some sign of guilt or panic at the understanding that his son had overheard what he'd said.

But Mr. Matthews's face was blank, and after a second he turned back around. "Yeah, I'm still here," he muttered into the phone.

Ken swallowed hard, clenching and unclenching his fists. The doorbell rang again, but Ken couldn't tear himself away from his father.

"Try Caruso," Mr. Matthews grumbled. "If he can't do it, then I'll be there." He slammed the phone into its cradle, then slowly turned to look at Ken.

"You have some nerve, listening in on a private conversation," he snapped, raking a hand through his thinning hair.

"How was I supposed to avoid it?" Ken demanded, feeling anger begin to replace the hurt. "You weren't exactly trying to keep your voice down." He

20

narrowed his eyes. "Tell me why you don't want to cover the game."

Mr. Matthews's jaw twitched. "I've got other plans," he said curtly.

Ken let out a choke of angry laughter. "Right." He shook his head and glanced down.

"Do you want to hear me say it?" his dad asked.

Ken kept his eyes trained on the floor. He kicked at the faded gray carpeting that lined the hallway.

"Fine," Mr. Matthews continued. "I'm not exactly looking forward to watching my son ride the bench."

Even though he'd known what his dad would say, the words burned through Ken, searing him like acid. His head jerked up, and he glimpsed a flash of remorse on his dad's face, but before his dad could say another word, Ken spun around and took off for the front door, yanking it open without taking a second to try and calm down.

Maria stood there, looking absolutely beautiful in her white tank top, red shorts, and running shoes. The girl could make a bathrobe look like high fashion. But something was off, something was missing. . . .

Her smile, Ken realized. Maria was frowning at him, her dark eyebrows scrunched together in concern.

"Is everything okay?" Maria asked, peering around Ken into his house. "It sounded like someone was yelling. . . ."

Ken stepped through the door and slammed it

behind him. He squinted as he stared down the street, avoiding Maria's gaze.

She placed her hand on his upper arm, and the softness of her touch sent ripples of warmth through Ken's body.

"Were you guys fighting again?" she asked gently.

Ken's breath caught, and he couldn't answer, but he lifted his head and let it drop again in a slight nod. "Let's just go," he said gruffly. "We can talk about it later."

Maria gave his arm a brief squeeze and then let go, and they started to jog down the sidewalk next to each other. All Ken wanted right then was to run hard enough to forget that football, his dad, and maybe even *he* ever existed.

Elizabeth shot straight up in bed when she realized the sound she'd been hearing while half asleep was the phone ringing.

Conner. The name flashed through her brain and sent her pulse racing. She jumped up and ran over to her desk, quickly snatching up the receiver midring.

Please be him, please be him.

"Hello?" she blurted out.

It was amazing she'd even slept at all last night—she'd been so worried about what had happened to Conner after he left The Shack drunk out of his mind. And she had been so devastated by the harsh insults he'd thrown at her before bolting.

"Liz?"

The disappointment washed over her, and she sank down into her desk chair.

Not Conner.

"Hey, Liz, it's Evan."

"Hey," she managed to reply. Then suddenly she clutched the phone tighter. Evan had left with Conner last night. Which meant that—

"Is Conner okay?" she asked, pushing her blond hair back out of her face. "What happened?"

"He's okay," Evan said. Elizabeth let out a breath she hadn't known she was holding, and her grip on the receiver loosened a notch.

"I was so scared. I mean, the way he just went off on me in front of the club," Elizabeth started to babble, "and he was so drunk and he actually wanted to *drive* and the things he said . . ." She stopped, feeling the pain all over again at how Conner had shoved her away on a night that had been so important to him, to both of them, when all she'd done was try to be there for him. Like always.

"So, um, you haven't heard from Conner yet this morning, then?" Evan asked. Elizabeth immediately recognized the fear in his voice, and her heart started to pound all over again.

"Why?" she almost whispered. "What aren't you telling me?"

Evan took in a deep, audible breath.

Elizabeth started to drum her fingers on the surface

of her wood desk. "You're starting to freak me out here, Evan."

"I know—I'm sorry," Evan said. "Really. It's just . . . I know he's going to be annoyed that I told you anything."

At least he's capable of being annoyed, Elizabeth tried to reassure herself. That meant he wasn't lying in some ditch on the road somewhere.

"Evan, you called me because you *want* to tell me," Elizabeth prodded.

"Yeah, you're right," he admitted. "But I think we need to do this face-to-face."

Elizabeth gritted her teeth. "I can be at House of Java in fifteen minutes," she said, remembering that last night her brother, Steven, had offered to give Jessica a ride to work this morning. If anything had changed and her twin had taken the Jeep they shared, then Elizabeth would just find another mode of transportation. This was too important.

"No," Evan said. "Make it the Eggshell. I don't want to run into anyone we know."

"The Eggshell. Fine. See you there."

Elizabeth slammed down the phone, dashed to her dresser, and pulled on the first pair of jeans she could find. She rummaged through her shirt drawer, grabbed a faded gray T-shirt, then ran to the bathroom to brush her teeth. She was moving so quickly, she almost choked herself with her toothbrush. A million horrible possibilities kept rushing through her mind, and she couldn't seem to get anything done fast enough.

She practically had to remind herself to breathe.

Jessica watched, mesmerized, as the large, gleaming cappuccino machine came to life, whirring and whooshing the milk and air inside. Normally the noise drove her crazy—she'd memorized the pattern of sounds, and sometimes they played in her head when she was working on homework or trying to get to sleep. But right now she was happy for the distraction, relieved to have something to focus on aside from the mush of confusion in her brain.

She'd never thought about it before, but it was really pretty interesting how much effort it took to create something as weightless and insignificant as foam.

"Uh, miss?"

Jessica blinked, then turned back to face the counter. A slim, dark-haired woman who'd just bought a latte a couple of minutes ago was standing next to the guy waiting for his cappuccino. She was holding her turquoise mug out to Jessica, frowning.

"I asked for chocolate," she said. "This has cinnamon."

"Huh?" Jessica bit her lip, trying to process the woman's words. "Oh. Right. Sorry. Hang on a sec, and I'll make you another one."

Jessica heard chuckling from the other end of the

counter. She shot a quick glance out of the corner of her eye and saw Jade smirking at her.

The woman rolled her eyes. "Never mind," she said. "I'm in a hurry."

"Oh," Jessica replied, flustered. "Okay. Then here, let me give you a coupon for a free drink next time you come." She searched around for her order pad and a pen, then quickly scribbled down the note, signing her name at the bottom.

The woman took the scrap of paper and walked away without even saying thank you. Jessica sighed. This day was *not* improving.

She turned to finish the cappuccino, then handed it to the guy waiting and leaned back against the wall, relieved that there were no new customers.

She was just about to do a check of the napkin dispensers at the tables when she heard the jangle of the door opening, and she glanced over automatically to check who was coming in.

When she saw who it was, Jessica froze, and her arms fell limply at her sides.

Jeremy.

Jessica took in his slightly messy brown hair and the sweet, vulnerable expression in his deep brown eyes. He was wearing a pair of faded jeans with a Big Mesa T-shirt. Not the usual khakis and button-down shirt.

Jessica realized that he really was a mess from last night. *Crushed* was the word Jade had used, wasn't it?

Jessica quickly checked to see Jade's reaction. But Jade wasn't where she'd been a second ago. Jessica searched the room, spotting Jade in the back corner, clearing off the table in one of the cushy booths. She hadn't seemed to notice Jeremy.

Jessica turned back to see Jeremy. He was heading straight toward her. Her cheeks flushed, but she didn't look away. She held her breath as she examined his face closely to figure out if he was about to lay into her all over again. She didn't think she could take it.

As he got closer, Jessica instinctively reached out and grasped the edge of the counter for support.

"Hey, Jess," he said softly.

She took a shaky breath. "Hi."

Hi? Jessica berated herself. Was that the best she could come up with after giving him a front-row seat to watch his girlfriend cheat on him last night?

Jeremy stuffed his hands into his pockets, shifting awkwardly.

"Uh . . . I just wanted to say that I'm sorry," he muttered.

Jessica had to press her palms hard against the countertop for support. Had *he* just apologized to *her?* "What?" she choked out.

Jeremy looked away from her, peering into the glass case next to the counter. He was staring at the biscotti and muffins inside as if they held the secrets of the world. "I shouldn't have said that stuff

27

to you last night." He paused. "I was way too harsh."

Surprise and relief surged through Jessica, and the cold knot that had formed in her stomach began to relax. "Really?" she asked, her eyebrows raising hopefully.

"Yeah, really." He took his hands out of his pockets and ran his fingers along the counter. "I guess I just didn't want to see that, you know?" he said. He glanced over at Jade, and Jessica followed his gaze. Jade was still immersed in wiping down the table. She seemed to be scrubbing pretty hard, actually, Jessica noted.

Jeremy turned back to face Jessica, and it killed her to see the amount of pain in his adorable, soft eyes.

"So anyway, that's all," Jeremy said. "I'm just . . . sorry." His voice cracked on the last word, and something told Jessica that he wasn't simply apologizing to *her*. The guy's heart was breaking. He sounded the way he had back when he and Jessica had broken up.

Did he really like Jade that much? Jessica wondered. She swallowed, a bitter taste rising to her mouth.

"So, are we okay?" Jeremy asked her.

Jessica smiled for the first time that day. "Yeah, we're okay," she replied. His hands were still resting on the counter, just a few inches from hers, and she moved her fingers slightly so that their fingertips touched. An unexpected spark rushed through her, and a blush crept over her cheeks again.

"Good," Jeremy replied. He pulled his hands away, stuffing them back in his pockets. "So we're still friends."

"Friends," Jessica echoed, feeling a strange chill. "Right." The word had never sounded so hollow to her before.

"Except there is one thing," Jeremy said, his brow furrowing. He leaned in toward her, and her heart jumped.

"What's that?" she asked, hoping with every fiber of her being that this no-customer stretch would continue long enough for her to hear whatever Jeremy had to say.

"I think I need to find a new job," Jeremy said.

Jessica's mouth dropped open. "Wh-Why?" she stammered. She didn't even care if she sounded like an idiot—the idea of Jeremy leaving HOJ was utterly unreal.

Jeremy shrugged. "Me, you, and Jade all working here together? It's a minefield, Jess."

A minefield?

Jessica turned her back on Jeremy to restack the coffee filters, worried that Jeremy would see the absolute panic in her eyes. Her mind raced as she tried to figure out how to talk Jeremy out of this.

"Jess? What are you doing?"

Jessica flinched, then noticed that she'd left the milk carton out of the minifridge. "Just straightening things," she said, walking over and placing the carton in the compact refrigerator that sat beneath the coffee machines.

"Jess?" she heard Jeremy call.

"I'm almost done," she answered, remaining in her kneeling position.

"Uh, you have a customer," he said.

Jessica bounced back up and faced the counter. One of the regulars, an older guy with thinning gray hair and his usual newspaper, stood waiting next to Jeremy.

"Sorry," Jessica apologized, quickly pushing away the strands of blond hair that had escaped her ponytail. "Regular coffee, with milk and sugar?" she asked, repeating his normal order.

The guy nodded. "And a blueberry muffin," he added.

Jessica went to work preparing his drink, relieved at the opportunity to stall Jeremy a little longer.

Unfortunately, it wasn't exactly a time-consuming beverage choice. As she took the man's money and made change, she noticed that her hands were shaking slightly.

"Look, I should go," Jeremy said once the man had wandered away to a nearby table. "I guess Ally's not around?"

"No, she's not here yet," Jessica responded, feeling

herself enter the total-panic stage. "But wait," she blurted out. "I mean . . . okay, so maybe it won't be easy for you to work with Jade anymore." Jessica snuck a quick peek in Jade's direction, and this time she caught Jade watching them. Jade immediately turned away, but Jessica was pretty sure she'd seen a glimmer of hurt in Jade's eyes. *Not possible,* Jessica told herself. Jade had proved how heartless she could be. She was probably just still annoyed that she'd been caught.

Suddenly an idea came to Jessica. It would solve everything—for Jeremy *and* for her, conveniently. She leaned over the counter again, licking her lips. "*She* should be the one to quit," Jessica suggested. "You need this job. And you've been working here longer." She frowned. "You've got—what's that called? Tenure."

A flicker of a smile passed over Jeremy's lips. "Jess, I'm a waiter, not a college professor."

Jessica let out an exasperated sigh. "Whatever. You know what I mean. Why should you have to leave just because Jade's a total . . ." Jessica trailed off when Jeremy took in his breath sharply, his eyes looking even more wounded than she'd thought possible. Obviously Jeremy wasn't ready to hear Jade blasted, even after what he'd seen last night. Did it make Jessica a selfish monster if that bothered her more than the simple fact that Jeremy was hurting?

Jeremy glanced around the room, then back at

Jessica. "I can find something else," he said softly. "It's easier that way, you know?"

Easier? How could anything about this be easy for Jeremy when Jessica felt like the earth itself was shifting around underneath her? He *couldn't* leave—it just didn't work that way.

"So this is it?" she squeaked, unable to comprehend what was happening. "No more working together?"

No more working together meant no more *seeing each other*, didn't it? It's not like they went to the same school or anything. How could Jeremy even consider this? Wouldn't he . . . miss her?

"Uh, so can I have some paper?" Jeremy asked, ignoring her question. "I just want to leave a note for Ally."

"Right," Jessica said, nodding slowly. Somehow she couldn't seem to move to grab the blank order pad lying on the ledge behind her.

Jeremy gave her a funny look, then reached over and took the pad himself, along with a nearby pen.

As she watched him scribble his note to Ally, Jessica had the crazy thought that maybe she should tackle him—slam him to the floor to keep him from leaving. Of course, since he was a good fifty pounds heavier than she was and an experienced football player, she probably wouldn't even be able to budge him, let alone knock him down.

"You know, you can't quit in a note," Jessica

pointed out, aware of the urgent pitch of her voice. "It's—It's like breaking up with someone over the phone."

Jeremy glanced up from the pad, giving Jessica another strange look, like she didn't speak English or something. "I know," he said. "I'm just telling her to give me a call so we can set up a time to talk."

Jessica winced, then forced a fake smile as two men in dark suits approached the counter.

"Can I help you?" she asked the men.

"I'll have a large double-mocha decaf," one of them said as he straightened his suit jacket.

"Sure," Jessica said, reaching for a cup. She nodded at the second man.

"Hot tea. Lemon, no sugar," he said.

Jessica turned to fix their drinks, keeping Jeremy in her peripheral vision the whole time. She was still trying to think of a way to talk him out of this—something she'd missed.

She wondered what the two suit guys would think if she suddenly hurled herself into Jeremy's arms and begged him not to quit, latching herself onto him without letting go until he agreed to stay.

She finished the coffee, then plunked a tea bag into a cup of hot water and turned to deliver the order.

"Here you go," she announced brightly, taking the crisp bills they held out to her and ringing them up.

As soon as the men walked away, Jeremy lifted his note. "I'm just going to leave this on Ally's desk," he explained, pointing toward the employee lounge in the back. "Um, I guess I'll see you around, okay?"

Jessica's throat tightened, but she managed to nod as she watched him disappear into Ally's office.

How would Jeremy "see her around" if he wasn't going to *be* around? This whole thing was insane, like her life had just entered some kind of warp drive and things were happening around her too fast to control. First Jeremy dating Jade, then last night's disaster, and now . . .

She walked around the counter and sank down into a chair at an empty table a couple of feet away. This was hitting her *hard*. Harder than she ever would have expected.

But it's Jeremy, she found herself thinking automatically. And suddenly everything was very clear.

Jade Wu

One of the things I liked best about Jessica Wakefield was that it seemed like she knew how to have a good time. Looks like I was way wrong on that one.

So I fooled around with Josh a couple of times while I was going out with Jeremy. So what? I mean, am I supposed to give up my whole social life just because a guy bought me dinner and kissed me a couple of times? Okay, they were <u>great</u> kisses, but I wouldn't know that if I didn't have anything to compare them to anyway, right?

Maybe it's just that Jessica can't handle when someone else has a little fun. But you know what? I think her little stunt last night messed up her life a lot more than it messed up mine.

Ken sucked the air into his lungs, forcing it out again in long rushes. He could feel a trickle of sweat gliding down his back between his shoulder blades, and his leg muscles tingled. It was a great feeling to be able to outrun his anger. By the time his feet hit the corner of Main Street, he'd calmed considerably, and he began to slow down.

Beside him Maria slowed as well. Ken glanced at her out of the corner of his eye, smiling at the intense expression of concentration on her face. She wiped the perspiration off her forehead with the back of her slender hand, her breathing still coming out evenly. Ken loved to watch Maria run—she seemed so *natural*.

Ken winced as he remembered the way his dad had used that word in the past to describe the way Ken looked on the field, throwing passes. *You're a natural, kid*, his dad would tell him, beaming that ridiculously proud grin.

Ken continued to ease his pace so that he was practically walking, and Maria did the same. He

37

shook his head, trying to push away his thoughts. So his dad was ashamed of him. It was time he got over it. It's not like he'd been so impressed with his dad lately either. Mr. Matthews had been acting like a serious dirtbag, treating perfectly nice women with no respect. Ken tilted his head from side to side, stretching the tension out of his neck and shoulders.

Maria stopped and lunged forward to stretch out her legs. "I could use some water," she said. "Are you ready for a break?"

Ken turned to face her, focusing on her amazingly beautiful eyes and soft, appealing lips. If only he could just spend all his time staring at Maria, then it would be tough to let all those ugly, angry thoughts in.

"Yeah, water works for me," he said. His throat was feeling pretty dry. But the last place he wanted to go was back home. "Why don't we head over to House of Java?" he suggested, scratching his head. "It's pretty close."

Maria glanced down the street, shading her eyes from the bright sun. She nodded. "Okay, let's go," she agreed.

They rounded a corner, and Ken relaxed as the light breeze blew over him. Then suddenly he saw something that made him stop dead in his tracks.

"Ken—what's wrong?" Maria asked, frowning up at him. Then she followed his gaze across the street and let out a small sigh. She linked her fingers through his, and the softness of her skin helped him keep from totally flipping out.

Will Simmons, wearing a suit and *tie,* was heading into Chez Lorraine, a fancy restaurant down the block from HOJ. Melissa Fox was at Will's side, clinging to his arm and beaming her cheerleader smile. Behind them were Will's parents, and next to Will's dad was the reason for Ken's reaction: Hank Krubowski, the University of Michigan scout. Ken had met the guy junior year. He could still remember the encouraging praise he'd received from the scout—the promise of things to come. Of course, that was before Ken lost his starting position on the team. To Will.

Ken squinted at the happy little group. So it was a done deal, then. They were probably out celebrating Will's acceptance to Michigan, his football scholarship, his whole damn perfect life.

Ken's head swam as he watched Hank step forward to hold open the door for the rest of them. Mrs. Simmons and Melissa glided through the entrance together, then Hank flashed Will a worshipful smile, and Mr. Simmons clapped his son on the back before the three men sauntered into the restaurant.

Ken couldn't help imagining that it was him walking through that door with Mr. Krubowski, flanked by proud parents and an adoring cheerleader girlfriend. But somehow Will was disappearing into Chez Lorraine with Ken's life—Ken's future.

Maria let go of Ken's hand and gave him a playful whack on the shoulder. "Hey," she said, smiling. "As soon as you're done plotting the guy's murder, I could go for some water, okay?"

Ken frowned and started walking again, though his legs suddenly felt tired.

"I know it's rough to see that," Maria said quietly. "It seems like Will's got everything happening. But you know what?" She glanced up at Ken, her brow furrowed thoughtfully. "In the end, talent always survives. And you've got talent." Her features softened into an encouraging smile. "Things will work out for you, Ken. I know they will."

"Thanks," he replied, genuinely affected by her words. It was crazy—ever since Ken had gotten to know Maria in the beginning of the year, she'd believed that he could do things that seemed impossible. And it wasn't because he was a star athlete or anything like that. It was just because he was . . . Ken.

Maria's smile widened, and she tossed back her head. "That's what girlfriends are for, right?" she teased.

"Actually," Ken said, reaching out to pull her to him, "I thought *this* was what girlfriends were for." He pressed his lips to hers in a soft, deep kiss, savoring the tingles that ran down his spine, then gently pulled back, keeping his arm around her small waist.

"Yeah, well, that too," Maria said with a laugh. "Come on, let's go." She took his hand again and started dragging him toward House of Java.

Was it possible that Ken had just been envying Will? So what if Will had the perfect all-American life waiting for him—Ken had something better. He had Maria, and he would never trade her for Will's cheerleader girlfriend. Maria was sweet, smart, and *real*—and also a total knockout.

And most important, somehow when Maria told him things would be okay, Ken believed her.

Will carefully placed his light blue silk napkin in his lap, then reached under the table and gave Melissa's knee a squeeze. She gently swatted his hand away but smiled at him, her blue eyes gleaming.

Glancing across the table, Will saw that his mom was still studying the menu. Next to her, Will's dad and Mr. Krubowski were speaking softly about life in Sweet Valley.

Will nervously straightened his lucky paisley tie, the one Melissa had given him for Valentine's Day last year. He helped himself to a roll from a silver platter in the center of the table, then broke it in half on his butter plate. A few crumbs fell onto the tablecloth, and he quickly scooped them up to put them back on his plate. Will wasn't used to going to restaurants like this, and he kept worrying that he'd do something to cause Mr. Krubowski to say that he really wasn't Michigan material.

You're being ridiculous, Will told himself as he

leaned back in his chair. *Hank recruited you because of what you do on the field*. Table manners weren't part of the application process.

A tall waiter wearing a crisp tuxedo walked over to take their orders, and Will let everyone around him go first. His mom and Melissa both chose Belgian waffles, and his dad and Hank got omelettes.

"And for you, sir?" the waiter finally asked Will, standing over him with his pen poised over his pad.

"Uh . . . I'll have a mushroom-and-cheese omelette," Will said. "With sausage and hash browns on the side. Oh, and a buttered bagel too."

As soon as the waiter walked away, Mr. Krubowski let out a deep laugh. "He certainly eats like a Division I football player!"

Mr. Simmons shook his head, grinning. "Good thing you're getting a full ride, son," he teased. "The cost of your meal plan alone would break us!"

"Bill!" Mrs. Simmons interjected, her eyelids fluttering in embarrassment.

Will exchanged a nervous glance with Melissa, and she smiled at him reassuringly. Just knowing she was here made this so much easier.

"So, shall we have a toast?" Hank suggested, raising his water glass. "To Michigan's newest star quarterback!"

Melissa raised her orange juice, her manicured nails making a small *ting* sound as they hit the crystal glass.

"To a successful athletic *and* academic career," Mr. Simmons added as he lifted his glass.

There was a brief silence as they all drank to Will. Then Mr. Simmons placed his elbows on the table and laced his hands together, staring at Mr. Krubowski intently.

"Speaking of academics," he began. "I was wondering if you could tell us a little more about the program of study at Michigan."

Will shifted uncomfortably in his seat. "Dad," he said. "We've been over that. I'm gonna take a generalized class schedule until I declare a major."

"Right," Hank agreed, nodding. "Mostly liberal-arts classes. We encourage our incoming freshman players to take a low-pressure course load. It gives them more time to focus on their sports commitment."

A worry crease appeared on Mr. Simmons's forehead. "I was under the impression that his first commitment was to his education," he said.

"Well, of course it is," Mr. Krubowski said. He was still smiling, but something about his smile seemed forced, and Will felt his palms start to sweat.

"Football is important to me, Dad," Will said, gripping the edges of his chair under the table. "It's why I chose Michigan in the first place." He fixed his father with a hard stare, hoping he'd get the message. "And it's why they chose me."

"We understand that, Will," Mrs. Simmons said.

"And we're very excited about your football career. But the point your father is making is that a sound academic background is also crucial."

Will glanced at Mr. Krubowski. The Michigan scout was toying with his fork, flipping it around in one hand. Will restrained himself from groaning. He knew his parents were right about his education being important. But Hank needed to believe that Will was prepared to eat, sleep, and breathe football for Michigan. Which he was. He'd had a lifetime of balancing sports with his classes, and he knew he could handle it at college too.

"Can you tell us about the matriculation policy at Michigan?" Will's father asked.

Will felt his gut tighten. He was going to wind up with a degree from one of the best universities in the country, and it wasn't going to cost his parents a cent—what difference did it make if he earned a few credits in basket weaving?

Will had to grit his teeth to keep from snapping at his dad to back off. His eyes shot back and forth between his father and Hank as he tried to figure out what to do. He felt a stab of panic as he worried that his dad would call off this whole thing, forbid him to go to Michigan because he didn't believe Will would be able to devote time to his education there. Will could see the vein throbbing in his dad's temple, the one that always signaled a meltdown.

Just as he was about to completely lose it, Will

felt Melissa's hand close around his under the table.

"Will and I have talked about this a lot," Melissa said in her sweet, perfectly pitched voice. Just the sound of it sent waves of calm over Will. "He knows that football and academics go hand in hand, and he'll find the right balance." She paused, flashing her confident smile first at Will's dad and then at Mr. Krubowski, both of whom seemed to visibly relax. "We'll make it work," she continued. "Together. We always have."

Mr. Krubowski returned Melissa's smile, and this time it looked genuine. Melissa had that effect on people—when she wanted to. Will felt his grip on the sides of his chair loosen.

"I apologize if I sounded hesitant," Mr. Krubowski told Will's dad. "It's just that I'm not used to parents—uh—*inquiring* about the curriculum. To be honest, it's kind of refreshing. Impressive, actually." He turned his focus to Will. "Your family is very grounded, very sensible—another reason you'll be a great asset to our school."

Will felt Melissa give his hand another squeeze, then she released it so he could shake the hand Hank was offering across the table.

"Thank you, Mr. Krubowski," Will said, a rush of excitement surging through him. This brunch could have been a serious disaster if it hadn't been for Melissa. But Melissa managed to keep everyone from going over the edge, as always.

Will glanced at Melissa, then down at his lucky tie. Turned out he hadn't needed the tie after all.

Elizabeth burst through the glass doors to the Eggshell and scanned the restaurant for Evan. The frustration built up inside her as she glanced from table to table. Of course she'd hit every red light on her way over here, and she didn't think she could wait even a second longer to know what was wrong with Conner.

Finally Elizabeth spotted Evan in a booth next to a window by the back. His head was bent over as he looked down into his coffee, his long, dark hair covering his face. She wove through the maze of Formica tables, the strong aroma of home fries and hot coffee making her nauseous.

When she reached the booth, Elizabeth slid in across from Evan and took a deep breath. "Okay, I'm here," she blurted out. "Now tell me what's going on."

Her heart hammered in her chest as she studied Evan's expression, trying to find a clue to how bad the news would be.

Evan stirred his coffee, then leaned back against the plastic booth, frowning. "Last night at the beach," he began, "Conner kind of . . . fell."

Elizabeth's head jerked back slightly in surprise. "Fell?" she repeated. "I don't—I don't understand." She shifted slightly on the hard seat, her legs itching from the thick material of the old jeans she'd thrown on.

46

So Conner fell—they *were* on the beach. What was the big deal?

Out of the corner of her eye Elizabeth glimpsed a waitress heading toward them, a redheaded girl around Elizabeth's age. "Um, we need some more time," she said.

The waitress shrugged her scrawny shoulders, then walked back in the other direction.

Elizabeth turned to focus on Evan again. His mouth twitched nervously, then he let out his breath in a long rush.

"You know those rocks down at the end of Crescent Beach?" he asked. Elizabeth nodded. "Well, I guess he wasn't thinking straight or something." Evan stopped and glanced away from Elizabeth, fidgeting with the end of the ugly yellow curtains that partially covered the window next to their booth. "Anyway," he continued, "he climbed the rocks when we weren't paying attention. And then he, uh, he took a spill."

Elizabeth felt the color drain from her face, and her hand immediately flew up to her mouth. "Oh God," she whispered, swallowing several times as another, stronger wave of nausea came over her.

"No, Liz—he's okay," Evan said quickly. He sat forward, meeting Elizabeth's gaze head-on. "I promise you—he's okay. He just got pretty scraped up. His palms, especially. And when I came over, he was . . . he was out for a little while. You know, unconscious."

Elizabeth gasped, wondering if she could physically tolerate any more information before her entire body would cave in on itself.

"He passed out," she said. "So he hit his head?" she asked, her voice wavering. She started tapping her fingers on the table's surface, doing her best not to inhale the surrounding scent of food too deeply.

"I don't think so," Evan replied. His tone was firm and strong, a total contrast to Elizabeth's. She wished that somehow she could have that bizarre ability not to let her emotions take total control of her body. "I saw him fall, and he landed on his arms and hands, not his head. I'm pretty sure he just passed out from drinking too much. Liz, he was *really* loaded. Honestly, I think he was so numb from the alcohol that he didn't even feel the scrapes. But when he saw the blood, it was like, lights-out, man."

"Oh God," Elizabeth repeated. She pressed her hands to her temples, trying unsuccessfully to fight back all the *what ifs* that crowded her brain.

"He could have slid into the water," she mumbled. "He could have drowned. He could have . . ." She trailed off, the image of Conner flailing to stay above the fierce waves that pounded the rocky point of Crescent Beach filling her head. She imagined him going under, choking on gulps of salt water, and suddenly felt like she was choking herself.

"I kept telling him to slow down." Evan shook his head. "I knew he'd had enough. More than enough.

But he wouldn't listen. And when I said I was worried about him, it just made him mad."

Elizabeth knew exactly what Evan meant. She'd felt that same frustration last night, trying to reason with Conner after his gig when it was obvious he was out of control. Why couldn't Conner listen to his friends?

"He's got a problem, Liz," Evan stated. He focused more closely on Elizabeth's face, his deep blue eyes so intense that she squirmed uncomfortably. "It's lucky he didn't mess himself up worse last night. And I don't know how lucky he'll be next time."

Next time? Wouldn't falling off the rocks at Crescent Beach be enough to shock Conner out of his drinking?

"Liz, you need to do something," Evan urged. "He'll listen to you. You're probably the only one with a shot at getting through to him."

"I don't know," Elizabeth said hesitantly, pressing her lips together. "I mean, I'll try, but— "

"Good," Evan interrupted. He flashed the gleaming grin that Jessica had rhapsodized about to Elizabeth during the two seconds Jessica had dated Evan a while back.

He does have a nice smile, Elizabeth thought. It was even managing to reassure Elizabeth slightly.

She jumped up. "Thanks for calling me, Evan."

Evan's smile disappeared. "Where are you going? You didn't even get anything."

Elizabeth cringed, putting a hand over her queasy

stomach. "That's okay," she replied. "I'm not really hungry. And I need to talk to Conner."

Evan reached out and grasped Elizabeth's arm, pulling her gently back down into the booth. "I don't know if now's the best time," he pointed out.

"Why not?" Elizabeth asked, confused. "I mean, if he's really that messed up, we have to deal with this right away."

"Yeah, but—he's gotta be in one seriously ugly mood this morning." Evan let out a low whistle. "We're talking a world-class hangover."

Even though she knew Evan didn't mean it like that, Elizabeth couldn't help feeling annoyed at the way he described it like some sort of achievement. She hated when guys talked about getting drunk in that competitive kind of tone. She could still remember how she'd felt the morning after she'd let herself drink too much, and it was definitely nothing *she* was proud of.

Elizabeth chewed on her bottom lip, debating what to do. Maybe Evan was right, and it *was* a bad time to try and get Conner to face this. But at the same time a part of her didn't even care—she just needed to see him.

"You ready yet?"

Elizabeth glanced up and saw that the redheaded waitress had popped up beside their booth, holding on to her order pad and staring at Elizabeth with a bored, slightly irritated gaze.

Ready—yeah, she was. She was ready to see Conner.

"Oh—um, actually, I don't think I'm getting anything," Elizabeth said. She cast a quick glance down at her messy, unflattering outfit. She had a feeling Conner wouldn't notice what she was wearing now anyway.

"So, I'm going," she told Evan. "Thanks for calling me, okay? You did the right thing."

From the reluctance apparent on his face, Evan didn't seem to agree—but Elizabeth couldn't wait any longer.

"I'll let you know what happens," she promised him, pulling the keys to the Jeep out of her pocket.

Without waiting to hear Evan's response, Elizabeth whirled around and rushed out of the restaurant as hastily as she'd entered just a few minutes ago.

TIA RAMIREZ

To: marsden1@swiftnet.com
cc: mslater@swiftnet.com,
       lizw@cal.rr.com,
       ev-man@swiftnet.com,
       kenQB@swiftnet.com,
       jess1@cal.rr.com
From: tee@swiftnet.com
Re: School spirit

Hey, everyone,
   Don't forget to show up at our big game against Ridgefield tonight! That means all of you, not just Jessica and Ken. :)-

CHAPTER
The Latest Crisis

4

I wonder what he's doing right this second, Ken thought as he gazed out the window of House of Java, imagining he could somehow see all the way around the corner into Chez Lorraine. *Shoveling scrambled eggs into his smirking face, courtesy of the Michigan recruiting office's expense account?*

Ken sighed, settling back against the worn upholstery of his chair. Why couldn't he keep his mind off Will Simmons? Ken tore his gaze away from the window and glanced next to him at Maria, who was waving across the restaurant to Jessica. Maria's smile was so warm, so open. Again he wondered how he could let any of this other stuff get to him when he had her.

Jessica waved back, but her return smile seemed forced. Ken noticed that her apron was a little lopsided, and her chin-length blond hair was kind of a mess. Jessica held up a finger to indicate that she'd be right over, then turned and grabbed some biscotti out of the jar on top of the counter.

"She doesn't look so hot," Ken said, stretching his legs out in front of him.

Maria cocked her head, watching Jessica as she handed the biscotti to a couple at a table up front, then started to head back toward the two of them. "Yeah, you're right," Maria agreed. "I wonder what's wrong."

Ken shrugged. Maybe he was a jerk, but he wasn't really in the mood to hear about Jessica Wakefield's latest crisis. Yeah, she was his friend, but she had a real way with melodrama.

"Hey," Jessica greeted them, plopping down in the overstuffed chair across from Maria.

Ken tried to swallow, but the itchy dryness in his throat made it slightly painful. "So, um, can we get a couple of waters?" he asked Jessica.

Maria gave his foot a quick kick. "No rush," she assured Jessica. "You look like you could use a break."

Jessica nodded, wiping an arm across her forehead. "Yeah, it's been a rough morning," she said. She frowned as she glanced back at Maria. "Have you talked to my sister today?"

Maria shook her head. "No, but I was going to call her later. After the way Conner acted last night—I hope she's okay."

"Me too," Jessica said, sounding distracted.

Maria leaned forward, crossing one smooth, dark leg over the other. "Did something else happen?" she asked. "No offense, but you're sort of a mess."

Jessica squirmed, a sour expression coming over her features.

"Wait—is it something with Jeremy and Jade?" Maria pressed, keeping her voice down.

Ken held back a groan. He'd told Jessica last night not to get involved in that. If Jade was cheating on Jeremy, that was their deal.

"I kind of don't want to talk about it," Jessica muttered. She cast a quick glance behind her at Jade. Ouch. Probably big-time tension there.

"Just tell me—did they break up?" Maria's dark eyes gleamed with interest.

Ken let out another sigh. One of the things he loved about Maria was how much she cared about people, including him. But sometimes her need to be superinvolved in all of her friends' lives went a little overboard.

"Yeah, they did," Jessica replied. "Long story, okay?" She reached out to grab some pieces of trash lying on the empty table next to theirs, then crumpled up the papers and stuck them in her apron pocket. "Anyway, what's up with you guys?" she asked.

Ken stared down at the floor, unable to shake his sullen mood.

"Hey, Ken? You in there?" Jessica teased.

"Ken didn't have a great morning either," Maria told Jessica. She reached out and took Ken's hand, giving it a supportive squeeze.

Ken was grateful for the gesture—but he really wished Maria hadn't said anything.

Jessica immediately leaned in closer to Ken, pushing her hair back behind her ears. "What's the deal?" she asked.

There was no point in hiding it now, right?

"Basically, my dad admitted that he thinks I'm a total loser," he said with a small shrug. Ken believed in being blunt.

Maria's eyes registered surprise. He realized he hadn't admitted that much to her yet either. "It's no big thing, really," he protested. "It's just, you know, now that I'm not a football star like Will-the-earth-turns-around-me Simmons, I'm not worth much as a son, I guess."

Ken hated how self-pitying he sounded, but somehow the words had just slipped out.

"I'm sure your dad doesn't really feel that way," Maria argued. "He's disappointed, okay, but—"

"Look, I heard him asking his boss to let him off covering the Sweet Valley game tonight," Ken interrupted. "And he even told me, straight on, he's embarrassed. Of me."

Ken pushed against the arm of the chair with his free hand, shifting himself over.

"I have an idea," Jessica said with a sly smile. "Why don't you kick Will's arrogant butt? That'll certainly get your dad's attention."

Ken laughed, but he sensed Maria's body stiffen next to him.

"Jess, that's not what Ken needs to—"

"No, I think it's a great idea," Ken put in. "Although I have a feeling your motives are a little selfish," he added, grinning at Jessica. Will had trashed Jessica's reputation, then stomped all over her heart. He knew Jessica had her own reasons for wanting the guy to take a fall.

Jessica rolled her eyes. "Okay, so Will's not my favorite person. If I were a little bigger, I'd kick his butt myself."

"I wish you would," Ken said, tracing the pattern on the oriental rug under their table with his foot. "Because Will getting injured is probably the only chance I have of getting back in the game."

"Ken—you're not serious," Maria said. Ken looked over at her and saw the worry in her clear, dark eyes.

"I'm kidding," he defended. "It's not like I hate Will or anything. It just sucks that we happened to be born in the same hemisphere."

"I can't argue with that," Jessica muttered as she stood back up, straightening her apron. "Listen, I'd better get back to work. I'll bring you your waters, okay?"

"Sure. Thanks, Jess," Maria told her. As soon as Jessica walked away, Maria turned back to Ken. Her eyebrows folded together as she frowned at him. "This is just about your dad, right? I mean, you're okay with not being a big football star anymore, right?"

"Ouch." Ken smiled. "Yeah, of course." He picked at a splinter of wood on the side of his chair.

Up until recently, Ken really had been okay with being head benchwarmer. It wasn't the thrill of his life or anything, but it was enough.

The problem was, he wasn't sure it *was* enough anymore. And not just for his dad. Ken didn't know if it wasn't enough for *him*.

Jeremy dropped down on a bench outside the corner deli where he'd picked up a bottle of juice and a copy of the *Sweet Valley Tribune*. He sat back and unfolded the paper, flipping through the pages until he reached the classified section.

Help Wanted.

He stared at the paper, recalling the way those words used to rule his family's life back when his dad had been out of work. At least now he didn't need a job to help support his parents and his two little sisters—he just needed extra cash.

Still, Jeremy told himself as he started scanning the ads. *It'd be nice to find something that pays decently.* And he didn't really want to be a waiter either. Too hectic. House of Java was easier because it was just coffee and snacks, and there were different things to do around there. It wasn't just running back and forth between the tables and kitchen, carrying trays loaded down with food plates. Plus he'd gotten to know Ally pretty well, so his schedule was always flexible if he absolutely had to change a shift once in a while.

Stop it, Jeremy told himself, adjusting the paper on his lap. He had to leave House of Java, for all the reasons he'd told Jessica. There was no way he could deal with facing Jade all the time after what she did to him. And Jessica . . .

Well, he was just better off getting some space from both of them.

It was weird—somehow seeing Jade with that guy at the beach last night had brought back all the hurt he'd felt when Jessica ditched him for Will. It was like watching some kind of twisted, sick instant replay of your worst nightmare. Jeremy had really liked Jade, a lot. And he'd thought he was over Jessica, but maybe the wound from what she did to him wasn't as healed as he wanted to believe.

Focus, Aames.

Jeremy reached over and unscrewed the top from his juice, gulping down a few swigs before turning his attention back to the paper. This wasn't the time to dwell on his pathetic romantic life. He needed a new job, no arguments.

Running his finger down the list of jobs, Jeremy sighed. He knew Sweet Valley wasn't exactly a raging metropolis, but he'd figured there would be more opportunities than *this*.

Jeremy wasn't in the least qualified to be an auto mechanic. He couldn't see himself as a baker's assistant or a cabdriver. Dental hygienist? Negative.

He moved farther down the list, careful not to miss anything. Midway down the page, Jeremy choked on his juice as he burst out laughing.

Exotic male dancer—that was *not* happening.

His laughter faded as another ad caught his eye: *Fantasy Island Fun House Attendant. Good pay, many shifts available. Applicant must be good with children and have working knowledge of Skee Ball and video games.*

Jeremy and Jessica had ended up at Fantasy Island on their first date. Jeremy hated it when people threw the expression around, but it had really been one of the best nights of his life.

A small, wistful smile crossed Jeremy's lips as he remembered how happy he'd been at the silly kiddie arcade with Jessica that night. It was crazy—they'd probably had more fun with all the video games than the little kids surrounding them.

Job, Jeremy. Job!

Jeremy rubbed his palm on his thigh to wipe off the newsprint that had transferred onto his fingertips, then spread the paper out on the bench next to him, leaning over to inspect it more closely.

Nothing. Nothing that seemed worth it, at least. Was he really doing the right thing, giving up his job? He hadn't actually quit yet, officially.

Jeremy shook his head as he remembered how awful it had felt to step inside HOJ this morning. His eyes had been drawn right to Jade, and all he could think about was how much fun he'd been having with her, how much he'd believed that things would be different with Jade than they were with Jessica. Maybe he hadn't been completely over the pain of how things ended with Jessica, but he'd definitely been ready to move on with someone new. Ready enough to be hurt pretty badly when that someone betrayed him the same way.

Well, not *exactly* the same way. At least Jessica hadn't gone so far as to make out with Will until she and Jeremy were actually broken up. Jade had taken things that one extra step.

Jade, Jessica, Jade, Jessica . . .

Jeremy folded the paper and stood up, yanking at his jeans. This was ridiculous—he wasn't getting anything done here but wallowing.

On Monday he'd check out the community bulletin board at school. Sometimes local businesses posted help-wanted flyers there. Maybe that would turn out better than these classified ads.

Because the one thing becoming painfully obvious was that there was no way Jeremy could stay at House of Java.

Jessica breathed a small sigh of relief when Ken and Maria left House of Java. It wasn't that she didn't like having friends stop by when she was working, but the last thing she was in the mood for today was Maria's pressure to get all the details on everything.

Okay, maybe that's not the last *thing,* Jessica thought as she peeked at Jade, who was standing at the other end of the counter, cleaning out a cinnamon container. Jessica was getting really sick of Jade's nasty little gloating smiles, especially when *Jade* was the one who'd been humiliated and dumped last night.

Maybe now's a good time to check the napkin dispensers, Jessica decided, grabbing a couple of packages of fresh napkins out from under the counter. Anything to get as far away from Jade as possible.

Keeping her eyes averted, Jessica passed behind Jade and walked around the counter to start refilling the dispensers on the tables. Just then she spotted Ally flying by on her way back to the employee lounge.

Jessica froze as she remembered the note Jeremy had left on Ally's desk. She dropped the packages of napkins on an empty table and rushed to follow Ally.

Jessica burst into her boss's office as Ally was taking off her gray zippered sweatshirt and sinking into the chair behind her desk. Ally glanced up at Jessica in surprise, and Jessica quickly checked out the desk's surface, searching for Jeremy's note. Her eyes landed on a scrap of paper right next to Ally's hand.

"Jessica? Something wrong?" Ally asked, frowning.

Jessica sighed. "Um, did you read that yet?" she asked, pointing at the piece of paper.

Ally's frown deepened, and she picked up the note and quickly scanned it. "What's this about?" she asked Jessica, looking back at her. "Do you know why he needs to talk to me?"

Jessica shifted her weight from one foot to the other. "Um . . . yeah, I do," she admitted.

Ally sighed. "What, does he want more shifts again? I swear, the kid is a workaholic." She brushed some dust off her desk, then started straightening the piles of papers sitting next to her Princess phone.

"No, he—he doesn't want more shifts," Jessica said, her voice catching. "Actually, he doesn't want any shifts." She smoothed down her apron, giving herself an excuse not to meet Ally's eye and reveal just how much this was killing her.

Ally's mouth fell open slightly. "Are you trying to say that he—"

"Jeremy's going to quit," Jessica interrupted. She began to pace back and forth in the small space in front of Ally's desk. "That's why he wanted you to call him. He came by to do it in person, but you weren't here yet."

A huge crease appeared in Ally's forehead, and her lips pulled tightly together into a stiff frown. "I thought he was happy here," she said, leaning back in her chair. "And I know he needs the money. I don't understand. What happened that you're not telling me?" She fixed an intent gaze on Jessica, and Jessica felt her cheeks flush.

"H-He, um, he had a reason," Jessica stammered.

She stopped walking and glanced up at the board on the wall where the workers' shifts were posted.

"Enlighten me," Ally replied in her usual straight-to-the point way.

Jessica bit her lip, then turned to face Ally again. She walked over and sank into the corner of the old maroon sofa by Ally's desk, then started fidgeting with the fraying material on the sofa's arm. "It sort of has to do with Jade," she said quietly.

"Jade? What are you talking about?" Ally was still staring at Jessica with her hard, hazel eyes. The woman must have had police training or something.

"Look—do I have to spell it out?" Jessica blurted out, instantly turning bright red. "I mean, you know, things happen sometimes, and then they don't work out," she quickly added, hoping that was all the explanation Ally would need. She did *not* want to have this conversation with her boss.

Ally sucked in her breath. "I see," she said. She propped her elbow up on the desk and rested her chin on her hand, narrowing her eyes thoughtfully. "Well, that's a shame," she said. "I hate to lose such a good worker. Are you sure he won't change his mind?" she asked, studying Jessica.

Jessica let out a short laugh. It's not like she hadn't been spending her entire morning wondering the same thing. But there was only one solution she could come up with—and she didn't see Ally going for it.

Jessica crossed her legs, leaning forward. "Between you and me," she began, "Jade's really nuts. That's why Jeremy's so convinced he has to leave. You just never know what's coming next with Jade." Jessica paused, making sure she did this right. "You know, she's late for her shifts all the time, she disappears on these superlong breaks, and sometimes she's even obnoxious to customers."

"Really?" Ally asked, her eyes widening. At least Jessica had her interested.

Jessica nodded vehemently. "Yeah, and you want to know the worst? She called in sick, like, ten minutes before her shift began the night of her first date with Je—um, this time she had a date. Then she showed up *here* with the guy and laughed in my face over it."

"Jessica," Ally said. "These are some serious accusations you're making." She paused, her expression more serious than Jessica had ever seen it before. "Are you sure you're not just saying these things because of the situation with Jeremy?"

Jessica swallowed, feeling a twinge of guilt. She'd kind of exaggerated the stuff about Jade talking back to customers. But the last part had been totally true, and that was obviously affecting Ally the most.

"No, it really happened," Jessica answered, digging the toe of her shoe into the carpet.

"Well, why didn't you tell me this before, then?" Ally demanded. She got up and walked around her desk, standing right in front of Jessica.

Jessica felt her temperature shoot up, but she tried to stay calm. "You know, you just don't *do* that," she replied lamely.

"Oh, really? Actually, Jessica, assistant managers are supposed to report things like this," Ally snapped.

Jessica winced, feeling like she'd been slapped. "I'm telling you now," she almost whispered.

"Yes," Ally said, nodding to herself, her straight brown hair bobbing up and down. "So I have to figure out what to do with this information."

"It really is the truth," Jessica said, jumping up so that Ally wasn't towering over her anymore. She faced her boss, staring her right in the eye. "I'm sorry I never said anything when it happened, but I swear I'm not making it up."

Ally continued to nod. "I believe you," she responded. "I'd noticed a couple of things like that myself, but I figured since I hadn't gotten any complaints from the staff"—she stopped, giving Jessica a pointed glare—"that Jade was working out okay."

"So, then—what are you going to do?" Jessica asked, excitement starting to build up inside her. If Ally fired Jade, then Jeremy would have to take his job back!

Ally turned and walked back around her desk, pulling a sheet of paper out from one of the drawers. "Regardless of Jeremy," she said, "we have to let Jade go if she's really behaving like that. Showing up here on a date after calling in sick is inexcusable."

Jessica's heart jumped. *Yes.* It worked—she'd convinced her!

"*But* I also need a way to teach you more responsibility," Ally added. Jessica froze—was her job in trouble now too? "You need to understand that being an assistant manager puts you on a different level from the rest of the staff," Ally continued. "Part of your job is to watch over them and make sure they're doing what they're supposed to be doing."

"So, what are you saying?" Jessica asked cautiously.

"To start with," Ally said, "I think that *you* need to be the one to tell Jade she's fired."

Will Simmons

Best wishes, Will Simmons.
Sounds like a card I'd send my aunt.

Thanks for being a fan! Will
Simmons.
Kind of cocky.

Your friend, Will "The Chill"
Simmons.
Okay—way too dorky.

#12, Will Simmons.
I like it—short and simple.

Yeah, I know, college football
players don't usually sign autographs.
But college is only four years. Then
there's the NFL. It can't hurt to be
prepared.

Elizabeth tapped her left foot against the floor of the Jeep, her right foot pressed down on the brake. The second the light turned green, she released the brake and slammed down on the accelerator, sending the Jeep sailing forward.

It wasn't like getting to Conner's any sooner would change anything. She'd still find her boyfriend banged up from his fall last night, nursing a bad hangover. And most likely, he'd still push her away. But knowing that didn't make Elizabeth any less eager to see for herself that he was really okay.

Elizabeth let out a sigh of relief as she finally pulled up in front of Conner's house. Glancing down, she noticed that her knuckles were white from the death grip she had on the steering wheel. She shook out her fingers, trying to get the circulation to return, then turned off the engine and walked up to the front door to ring the bell.

Conner's mother answered the door within seconds, and Elizabeth immediately registered the worry in Mrs. Sandborn's clear blue eyes.

"Oh, Liz, I'm glad you're here," she said, stepping back so that Elizabeth could come in. Elizabeth's gaze flickered over Mrs. Sandborn's outfit, taking in the rumpled button-down shirt and worn jeans. It was obvious that Conner's mom wasn't having an easy morning.

"I've been trying to get Conner to come out of his room all morning," Mrs. Sandborn confessed as she led Elizabeth through the foyer to the stairs. "Maybe he'll talk to you."

"I hope so," Elizabeth muttered, straightening her sweatshirt. She flashed Conner's mom a quick, encouraging smile, then jogged up the stairs and headed right for the door to Conner's room.

"Conner?" she called out, knocking lightly on the white plaster door.

There was a long pause, then Elizabeth heard heavy footsteps and the door swung open, revealing Conner looking worse than she'd ever seen him before. Spikes of his short, tangled hair stood up in tufts all over his head, and the whites of his eyes were almost entirely red.

"You look terrible," Elizabeth whispered. She threw her arms around his neck, pressing her face against his chest. The familiar feel of his soft cotton T-shirt on her cheek was comforting, but she could smell the bitter scent of alcohol drifting down from his breath.

Elizabeth held on to Conner for a moment

longer, then slowly pulled back, glancing up at his face, even though what she saw there made her want to cry. "Are you okay?" she asked.

Conner's eyes darkened. "I'm fine," he said, avoiding her gaze. He reached his arm to run his hand through his hair, and Elizabeth let out a soft gasp as she saw that it was scraped raw.

He'd made some attempt to bandage it—a trail of tape and gauze pads covered his arm from the wrist to the bicep, but there were enough gaps between them to reveal the extent of the wounds. The palms of his hands were covered with deep scratches and cuts.

"Conner," Elizabeth said, trying to keep her voice even, "you're not fine." She touched one of the bandages and caught him flinching. "I think you could have used stitches."

Conner turned and walked back into his room, keeping his back to Elizabeth as he fidgeted with his dark bedspread. "I just got a few cuts," he said. "It's no big deal. If Will Simmons came off the football field like this, everyone would say he was a hero."

Elizabeth followed Conner into the room and sat down on the edge of his bed, facing him. "But this didn't happen because of football," she said evenly. "It's because you were drunk, Conner."

Conner's eyes darted nervously around the room, and he started pacing between the bed and his dresser. "I was a little buzzed, that's all," he mumbled.

"Evan said it was more than a little," Elizabeth argued, crossing her legs and leaning forward. It almost made her dizzy to watch Conner. Not a single part of him could keep still—every muscle seemed to be twitching as he paced.

"Evan should mind his own damn business!" Conner burst out, kicking the bottom drawer of his dresser in anger.

Elizabeth sucked in her breath. She clasped and unclasped her hands, twisting her fingers together as she tried to figure out what to say.

"Conner, I just want to help," she finally stated, trying to catch his eye with her pleading gaze. "I—I think maybe you have a problem," she said softly, hugging herself.

Conner finally stood still, directing a fierce glare at Elizabeth that seared right through her. "The only problem I have," he said, "is you."

Elizabeth tried not to let his words sting her, but she felt the tears press against the back of her eyelids.

"One mother, even a drunk, is enough," Conner continued, his green eyes flashing with bitterness. "I don't need anyone else to nag me. How many times do I have to tell you people? *I am fine.*"

Conner bellowed loudly enough for the neighbors to hear. Elizabeth glanced over at the door to his room. It was still open, so Mrs. Sandborn had probably caught enough to be seriously concerned.

Slowly Elizabeth moved her gaze back to

Conner's scratched-up arm. "It doesn't look that way," she said, mustering the courage not to back down and fall into sobs.

"Then maybe you should stop looking!" Conner yelled. "Just get out, okay? *Leave*." He stopped, a strange expression coming over his face. "No, you know what? Forget it. Stay if you want—I'm out of here." He rushed out of the room and down the stairs. Elizabeth heard Mrs. Sandborn calling his name, then the front door to the house slammed a second later.

Elizabeth pressed her lips together, unable to move. Finally she stood up and hurried out of his room, blinking back tears.

As soon as she was in the hall, Elizabeth started crying. She flew down the stairs, unable to even see where she was going through the haze of tears streaming down her face.

"Elizabeth? Honey, are you okay?"

Elizabeth stopped at the foot of the stairs, her breath coming out in gasps as the sobs subsided. She wiped her hand across her eyes, then looked up to see Mrs. Sandborn standing in front of her.

"He won't listen," Elizabeth managed to say, her throat tight from crying.

"I'm sorry," Mrs. Sandborn said. She rested her hand on Elizabeth's shoulder, giving it a light squeeze. "Thank you for trying. You have to understand that this isn't really Conner. It's all about the alcohol." She shook her head, and Elizabeth saw a flash of pain in her eyes. "Trust me," she said softly. "I've been there."

"But I don't understand," Elizabeth choked out. "How come I didn't see this sooner?" Just a few days ago Tia had warned her—she'd tried to convince Elizabeth that Conner was drinking too much. And Elizabeth hadn't listened. She hadn't wanted to accept that Tia could know Conner better than she did. What was the matter with her? Was she really that petty?

Elizabeth sank down onto the bottom stair. She sniffled as the tears finally dried up.

Mrs. Sandborn sat down next to her, pushing her curly hair out of her face. "You can't blame yourself," she told Elizabeth. "It doesn't work that way."

"Tia knew," Elizabeth muttered, picking at the worn carpeting on the stairs. "She said he was heading for trouble, but I didn't want to believe it." She took a deep breath, steadying herself. "Did you—did you see his arm?"

Mrs. Sandborn's face paled. "What do you mean?" she asked.

Elizabeth cringed. She didn't want to be the one to clue Conner's mom in on what Evan had told her, but she couldn't exactly backtrack now. "He scraped it up," Elizabeth said. "Last night, at Crescent Beach. He was drunk, and he—um, he fell over, I guess." Some kind of remaining loyalty to Conner kept her from revealing exactly *how* Conner fell.

Mrs. Sandborn's whole expression suddenly seemed eerily calm. "At least Megan's still at her friend's house," she murmured.

Elizabeth hadn't even thought to check if Conner's little sister was home, but she was relieved to hear that Megan wasn't around. Megan had been through a lot recently, and the last thing the girl needed was to watch her brother's meltdown. Plus Elizabeth knew Conner would hate himself even more later if he caused his sister any pain.

"So . . . what's next?" Elizabeth asked.

Mrs. Sandborn started nodding to herself, then stood up and wiped her palms against the sides of her jeans. "I think you should probably go home," she said to Elizabeth. "I really appreciate what you're doing, but when Conner gets back—I'd like to talk to him alone."

Elizabeth could see the seriousness in Conner's mother's eyes, and she knew that there wasn't anything more she could do. She just hoped that—for once—Conner would listen to someone who loved him.

Andy walked back into his room after getting up to brush his teeth and let out a long, deep sigh. He climbed onto his bed, propping his back up against the headboard and stretching his pajama-clad legs out in front of him.

This is really lame, he thought, gazing around his

room. It was Saturday, and Andy had nothing to do. Or nothing he felt like doing. He knew he should be cracking down on his homework, like he'd promised himself a million times lately. But somehow he just couldn't deal with calculus equations or history reading right now.

A couple of weeks ago he probably would have hopped out of bed and hit the speed dial to call Tia so they could go hang out at House of Java.

A couple of weeks ago I would have been making plans with Six too, Andy reminded himself, slowly sinking back down on the bed so that his head rested on his pillow.

It was pretty amazing how fast things could change. Andy had gone from having a girlfriend and a group of friends he loved to being more alone than he'd ever been in his life.

Annoyed with himself, Andy shoved aside his sheets and sat up again. He sounded like a twisted, depressing greeting card. He wasn't *alone*. He was just confused. Confused over realizing that he was gay and then discovering that none of his supposed close friends actually had a clue how to be there for him.

Andy glanced into his mirror, smiling when he caught sight of his messy morning hair. He made a face, relieved to be over that moment of pathetic self-pity.

Besides, Andy told himself, he was basing his

whole my-friends-suck theory on a few conversations—during which everyone had been absorbed in their usual melodramas.

Andy yawned, reaching his arms up high and filling his lungs with air. Just then he heard the phone ring, and he turned to glance at the black cordless receiver lying on his desk, narrowing his gaze as if he were staring down a potential enemy.

Should he pick it up? Andy hesitated, debating. Was there really anyone he felt like talking to right now?

That would be a negative, he thought, pressing his lips together. Well, except for Conner. But he had to do that in person.

Andy shrugged, deciding to follow his screening instinct. He left his room without even waiting to hear the message left on his machine, instead heading down the hallway to get in the shower.

Tia, or Liz, or whoever was trying to reach him to spill their problems would just have to deal. The Marsden help line was temporarily out of order.

"Remember what I said, okay?" Maria urged Ken, staring at him with wide, serious eyes. "At least *try* to talk to him."

Ken glanced behind him at the front door to his house, then back at Maria. "Yeah, I'll try," he lied.

Ken appreciated how Maria always tried to help, but sometimes her advice wasn't really on target. His dad wasn't exactly the kind of guy you sat down and "shared your feelings" with. But Ken knew the only way his sweet, caring girlfriend would relax was to reassure her that he would work things out with his jerk of a father.

"Okay, so I'll see you later," Maria said. She tipped her head up to his, and they shared a quick kiss.

"Mmmm," Ken said as he pulled away, grinning. "I can't wait."

Maria's smile widened, then she turned and jogged down his driveway.

Ken waited for her to disappear around the corner before he went inside, dread spreading throughout his entire body. Reluctantly he opened the door and stepped into the house, intending to go straight for the stairs and up to his bedroom. He slipped off his sneakers and stretched his legs out a little.

But before continuing, Ken heard the sound of the TV coming from his dad's den. And despite everything, he felt this crazy urge to go in there.

After all, he hadn't believed Maria when she'd told him that he had it in him to do better in school, but she'd been right. And without her constant pushing, he never would have kept trying to convince his coach to let him back on the team. But it worked, even if he was second-string now. So maybe she was right about his dad too—as unlikely as it seemed. Maybe Mr. Matthews felt as bad about their fight as Ken did, but he just didn't know how to say it. Ken knew what that was like, to have a tough time getting stuff to sound the way you meant it.

At least if he tried, he could tell Maria he'd done everything he could. Ken shrugged to himself, then headed in the direction of the den. As he got closer, he could hear that his dad was watching some kind of game. Ken blinked as he thought he recognized one of the familiar Sweet Valley High cheers. A lump began to form in his throat, but he crept closer until he was standing outside the same doorway he'd lurked behind earlier this morning, peering into the room.

The tape was bad quality, probably from someone's handheld video camera, but Ken instantly identified the footage from last week's game against North Arlington High. Ken watched silently as Will threw the beautiful pass that had broken the tie and led to Sweet Valley's ultimate victory against North Arlington.

The lump was now big enough to block Ken's throat completely, but Ken swallowed it back, then shifted his gaze to his dad. Mr. Matthews was perched on the edge of his leather couch, leaning forward, absolutely riveted to the screen.

For the second time that day Ken felt like he was going to be sick. He turned and stumbled up the stairs to his room.

At least he'd learned one thing—Maria's power to change his life had its limits.

*   *   *

Melissa finished carefully filling in the last *S* in Simmons, then dipped her paintbrush back in the red paint to dot the *i* and sat back to admire her work.

Will Simmons Is Dynamite.

Melissa had arrived at the SVH gym about twenty minutes earlier. Cherie, Gina Cho, Amy Sutton, and Lila Fowler got there right after her. Lila had brought a portable CD player, and the strong bass of the dance music vibrated through the gym floor.

"You should shake the brush at it," Cherie suggested from next to Melissa. "You know—spatter little red dots all over the background."

Melissa considered Cherie's suggestion, then scrunched her nose in disgust. She always liked her signs to be neat and precise, unlike the messy ones her friends produced. "I like it the way it is," Melissa said.

Cherie shrugged, stretching one long leg out in front of her as she bent over the banner she and Gina were working on together. Her black jeans were so tight, they seemed to be molded to her body. "I still think the spatter effect would be cool. It'll look like confetti."

"So why don't you use it on yours?" Lila suggested, glancing at Melissa and rolling her eyes.

Melissa smiled. It was fun having Lila around, watching her get in her little digs to the other members of the squad.

Cherie reached up to tighten her auburn pony-tail, then leaned across Amy and turned down the volume on the CD player. "So, Melissa," she said with a playful grin. "How was brunch with the 'in-laws'?"

"In-laws?" Gina sat back and raised her thin eyebrows questioningly. "Something you want to tell us, Liss?"

Melissa grinned. "Will had that Michigan scout eating out of his hand," she bragged. She dropped her paintbrush into the can of water, then leaned back, pulling her knees to her chest. "He couldn't stop talking about how happy he was to have Will in the program. We're going to have things really easy there."

"So, you're definitely going to Michigan too?" Gina asked. She accidentally dripped red paint on the gym's shiny floor and quickly wiped up the spill, then returned her attention to Melissa. "You're not applying to USC? You're just going with Will?"

Melissa frowned, wondering why her friends couldn't let this go. "Yeah, I'm *going with Will,*" she said. She cast a withering glance at Cherie and Gina's disaster of a banner. The letters were all mismatched shapes, and there were splashes of paint everywhere. It looked like something a kid in kindergarten would make. "Maybe you should start a new one," she said, letting her voice fill with the appropriate amount of disdain to humiliate them.

Lila let out a soft chuckle, but Cherie and Gina just pouted.

"I've heard that colleges give their sports stars all kinds of free stuff," Amy volunteered. She hopped up and strolled over to the bleachers to grab her black hooded sweatshirt, then pulled it on over her head and sat back down in front of her banner. "You know, like expensive cars or dinners at nice restaurants."

"I've heard they even have these girls who will do *anything* the guys want," Gina blurted out.

No one said anything, and Melissa stared down at the floor, her face growing tight with anger.

"I mean, obviously they don't need to do that for Will," Gina added quickly, laughing nervously. "Come on, Liss, I didn't mean it like that. I've just *heard* that they, you know, do that sometimes."

Melissa raised her gaze back up, her eyes narrowing into a steely glare, and Gina visibly shrank under the weight of the look. Melissa tried to hide the fact that her heart had started to pound against her chest. All she could think about was the way she'd felt when Will cheated on her with Jessica Wakefield. What if Gina was right? What if as soon as she turned her back or went home early one night to study, Will's coach took him to some party full of blond sluts who were just dying to get their hands on Will?

Melissa felt a chill pass through her. She jumped up, brushing her hands against her thighs. "I don't know why you're all making such a huge deal out of this," she snapped. "Will and I are perfectly happy together, and obviously you guys are just jealous because none of you can keep a guy interested for more than five minutes."

To Melissa's satisfaction, four stung expressions met her words. She walked over and grabbed her backpack, yanking out her cell phone. Quickly dialing Will's number, Melissa turned her back on her friends and headed over to the bleachers on the opposite wall.

"Hello?" Will answered after two rings.

"I miss you already," Melissa half whispered into the phone, tracing the bright white out-of-bounds line on the gym floor with her shoe.

Will laughed. "You just saw me an hour ago," he said.

Melissa bit her lip. She needed him to show her that her friends were crazy to doubt this.

"So what are you doing?" she asked.

I'm imagining how perfect our life will be when we're away from Sweet Valley and everyone who doesn't believe in us.

"Just checking out the Michigan playbook," Will replied.

"Oh." Melissa stiffened, then clenched her hands, her nails digging into her skin.

"And picturing you in a Michigan cheerleading uniform," he added warmly, "waiting to give me a big victory kiss after I win my first college game."

Melissa let out her breath, turning to face her friends. "Yeah, it's going to be great there, isn't it?" she said loudly. "You and me, at Michigan together."

"Yeah, of course," Will agreed. "Is everything okay?"

"Uh-huh, fine," Melissa responded, grinning widely. "I'll call you later." She clicked off the phone and sauntered back over to her friends, her confidence surging back.

After everything she'd been through this year, Melissa was finally getting what she'd always wanted. And there was no way she'd let her friends convince her of anything else.

Elizabeth Wakefield

The first haiku I ever wrote was in, like, fifth grade. I think it was about bike riding or ice-skating or something. Here's one from this morning:

Conner McDermott
Vulnerable and distant
Breaking my whole heart

Andy Marsden

"Yo, Conner, buddy, my man . . ."

"Hey, so, Conner, I don't know if you've heard it around, but . . ."

"Okay, let me first say that I promise to be the only one of our friends who isn't attracted to you, but you should probably know that . . ."

Why am I making such a big deal out of this? So I'm coming out to my best guy friend. It's just Conner. He's a little moody sometimes, but at least he's a reasonable guy.

CHAPTER

Attitude Adjustment 6

Stretching out across his bed, Will frowned in concentration at the Michigan playbook he was holding above his head. These plays were way more complicated than the ones he was used to at Sweet Valley or back at El Carro.

Will let his mind wander to that strange phone call from Melissa. She'd definitely been in superinsecure mode, but it didn't really bug Will the way it used to that Melissa needed some extra assurances once in a while. Maybe because he'd realized that he *liked* the way she depended on him.

Will plumped up his green pillow and stuffed it behind his head, turning his focus back to the playbook. He had to start now if he wanted to knock them dead when he got there next fall. He'd be a freshman, playing with star players from high schools across the country. Will was determined not to let any of them outplay him.

A soft knock on his door interrupted his study.

"Come in," Will called out.

The door opened, and Will's dad strode in.

He sat down on Will's wooden desk chair.

"Hey, Dad," Will said, placing the playbook face-down on the bed next to him. He tried not to let the disappointment show on his face—all he really wanted right now was to be alone with those plays. "What's up?" he asked, hoping this would be a quick father-son chat, though he wasn't really getting that vibe.

"I just wanted to check on how your history paper's going," Mr. Simmons said, running a hand through his thinning, dark blond hair.

Will blinked, then glanced at the surface of his desk, where his history text and notebook sat unopened just inches away from his dad's back.

"Oh, yeah. I'm still thinking some stuff out," Will replied.

Mr. Simmons frowned, crossing his arms over his chest. "It's due Tuesday, isn't it?"

"Yeah," Will answered, itching to return to the playbook. "I've got plenty of time."

"Well, I was thinking I could help," Mr. Simmons suggested, straightening his glasses. "Maybe we could surf the net for some information together. You said the paper's on the civil-rights movement?"

"Uh-huh," Will said, glancing at the playbook. "Listen, maybe tomorrow, okay, Dad? I have this big game tonight, and I'm trying to get psyched up." As soon as the words slipped out, Will instantly regretted what he'd said.

"Will, I think you need a little attitude adjustment here," his dad said, shifting slightly. "This is no time to be slacking off on your studies."

Will sighed. Actually, it was the perfect time to slack off. He'd been working hard for years now to keep everyone off his case. But he was already accepted to a great school—he was *in*. So why was his dad so worked up over one stupid essay?

"Dad, I could write this paper Monday and still get a good enough grade not to mess up my GPA," Will pointed out. He shoved himself up off the bed, then walked over to grab some dirty clothes from the floor and toss them into the laundry basket by his closet.

"Good enough?" Mr. Simmons demanded, standing up. "Since when do we settle for 'good enough' in this family? This is exactly what I was afraid of, Will. You can't rely on football to get you through everything. One day you won't be able to play anymore, and then you'll need a solid education to fall back on."

Will had heard this speech a million times, and he still couldn't take it seriously. The NFL was his future, not history papers.

"Dad, I'm going to a high-ranked university on a full scholarship. I think I've earned a break," Will said, plopping back down on his bed.

His father shook his head, then sighed. "Well, if you're not doing schoolwork," he said gruffly, pushing his glasses back up his nose again, "you can come outside and help me in the yard."

Will knew when not to push his luck. "Fine," he agreed, following his dad out into the hall and down the stairs.

"The grass needs to be cut, and the hedges could use a trim," Mr. Simmons said over his shoulder as they walked out to the front yard.

Even as he chopped away at the dead branches with his dad's hedge clippers, Will's mind stayed focused on the plays he'd been studying. He tried to imagine himself at Michigan, pulling off one of those killers—especially against enormous, topnotch opponents. How many times would he find himself flat on his back on the field? How many times would he get pounded into the dirt?

". . . all about developing character," his father was droning on.

Will turned away from the hedge. His father was beside him, picking up the clipped twigs and stuffing them into a plastic lawn bag. Will hadn't heard a word he'd said, but he figured it was nothing new anyway.

"Character is doing what you should do, not only what you have to do," his father continued. "It may look like you're coming into the homestretch, but actually, this is only the beginning. This is the chance to prove to yourself that you've got the determination to keep your grades up, even though you're accepted to Michigan. Staying power, Will. That's the true measure of success."

Will gave the clippers a violent squeeze, amputating another dry branch. "Dad, it's not like it's going to be a cakewalk when I get to college. I'm going to have to study my butt off there, not to mention practically killing myself to learn all those new plays."

His dad's eyebrows shot up. "What do you mean by that?"

"Nothing." Will let out a long rush of breath, then handed the hedge clippers to his dad. "You know something? You're right. I shouldn't be slacking off. I'm going inside to work on that history paper."

Will turned and headed toward his front door, though he had no intention of starting his history assignment. High-school classes were about to become part of the past. Michigan, his football career—they were the future.

"Hey, Simmons," Will heard someone call out. He whirled around and saw three of his teammates—Matt Wells, Josh Radinsky, and Jake Collins—hopping out of Matt's pickup. The next thing he knew, they were bolting across the lawn to gang tackle him and he was part of a tangled mass of muscular arms and legs and shoulders, tumbling over the grass.

Finally Matt rolled off and jumped up, followed by Josh. "Congratulations, man," Matt said, his hair full of leaves. "That's awesome about Michigan."

Will grinned, then went to stand up as Jake, who'd made first contact, began to drag himself to an upright position. But Will's right leg was awkwardly positioned under Jake's forearm, and as Jake released himself, Will felt his knee try to follow, twisting hard in the wrong direction. Will winced as pain shot through his leg.

"You okay, man?" Josh asked, reaching his hand out to Will. Will took it and let Josh pull him the rest of the way up, feeling his knee continue to burn as he stood. Will felt a flash of worry that he'd injured himself and wouldn't be able to play tonight, but after a couple of seconds the pain faded and his leg felt fine.

"So it's official?" Jake asked. "You're in?"

"Yep," Will said, his good mood returning. "Krubowski even gave me the playbook to study."

Matt shook his head, and some of the leaves drifted back to the ground. "You probably need a college degree just to figure out those calls, right? I bet they have some intense plays."

Will shrugged. "They're not that hard." *More like impossible,* he added silently.

"Not for you, maybe," Josh said. "You've got those QB brain cells."

"Yeah, and you'd better use 'em tonight against Ridgefield," Jake teased.

Will laughed. "That's the plan."

"Hey," Josh said, brushing dirt off his blue-and-gray-striped shirt, "after we kick some Ridgefield butt, why don't we go out and celebrate you going to Michigan?"

"Sounds good," Will said, casting a backward glance at his dad, who was busy clipping branches. He didn't seem to be paying attention to Will and his friends.

Or maybe he realized that I do deserve a break, Will thought, hoping it was true. His friends knew what a big deal his football career was—and soon enough his dad would understand that football was all Will needed.

Conner winced as the sound of the front door slamming behind him increased the throbbing in his head.

He hadn't really gone anywhere—he'd just driven around until he figured Elizabeth would be gone from his house. And luckily he'd timed it right since her car hadn't been in his driveway when he returned. All Conner needed was to go upstairs, climb back in bed, and get a little more sleep to dull the pain in his—

"Conner McDermott."

He froze, surprised at the flatness in his mother's unusually firm tone. He turned and looked into the living room, where her voice had come from. Mrs. Sandborn stood in the doorway, her face blotchy from an obvious crying spell but her eyes hard, determined. Focused.

"I want you to tell me what happened to your

arm," Conner's mother instructed, walking slowly toward him.

Conner sighed, then leaned back against the cream-colored wall. He glanced down at his bandaged arm, noticing that the tape was coming off one of the gauze strips. He reached his other hand over to press it down and keep the cut hidden, ignoring the pain that shot through him as he did so.

"I tripped," Conner mumbled, staring down at the hardwood floor of their hallway.

"Right," Mrs. Sandborn said. Conner hadn't realized that one word could be so heavy with sarcasm, but that one certainly was.

"Look, Mom, it's not a big deal," Conner said, pushing off the wall and starting to walk toward the stairs. "If you and Elizabeth would just—"

"Don't you think I know exactly what's going on?" Mrs. Sandborn erupted. Her carefully controlled tone had slipped into something more uneven, more . . . scared.

Conner stiffened as his mother approached him, pressing her hand down on his shoulder.

"Conner, I can help you," she pleaded, her voice cracking. "I've been there—I understand. I know you think things are under control, but they're not. Nothing is *ever* under control when you're drinking. Please listen to me."

Conner took a deep breath, then whirled around, shrugging out from her grasp. "Just because you're *weak*," he began, noting the hurt in her wide, blue eyes, "doesn't mean that I am. I'm not the drunk in this family. And until *you* have to come drag me out of some club where I've made a total fool out of myself and then hide me from Megan, I think you'd better leave it alone."

Mrs. Sandborn's eyes grew cold again, distant like they'd been when he first came in. "We can do this the hard way if you want," she warned him. "But it's ripping me apart to see booze do this to you, and I won't let it destroy your life like—like . . ." She stopped, dropping her head into her hands and falling back against the wall for support.

Conner recoiled. His mother was blaming herself for this supposed problem he had. He knew he should feel guilt or at least concern for her. But all he could muster was disgust that she crumbled so easily, like always. And anger that she'd lay this on him with everything he already had to deal with.

Conner shook his head, then walked up the stairs, his heavy footsteps blocking out the noise of his mother's tears.

Andy paused outside the door to Conner's house, staring closely at the small, round doorbell.

Finally he reached up and hit the button, listening to the *dingdong* that followed inside the house. Andy knew he was making way too big a deal out of this, but he couldn't help running through all kinds of crazy scenarios in his head. The worst was the one where Conner immediately pushed him out of the house, shouting something about "get out quick, before I catch it!"

So maybe Andy had been watching too many afternoon talk shows. Conner was probably the last guy in the world to say something so idiotic.

Andy shifted back and forth from one foot to the other while he waited for a response to the doorbell. He turned to make sure that Conner's Mustang was in the driveway like he'd thought. Yep, he wasn't imagining things.

Finally the door swung open, and Mrs. Sandborn stood there, her face full of weird red splotches.

Was she crying? Andy wondered, his discomfort increasing by the millisecond. Just like him to decide to announce his sexuality in the middle of some kind of family crisis.

Hey, Conner, Mrs. S.—sorry to hear about the aunt dying. But guess what—I'm gay!

"Hello, Andy," Mrs. Sandborn greeted. She stepped aside to let Andy in, and he walked inside, shuffling awkwardly.

"Conner's up in his room," Mrs. Sandborn told him, avoiding his gaze. "I don't know if he's up for company, but you can try." She paused. "I have to go pick up Megan and take her and her friends to the mall," she continued. "Do you think you'll be here for a while?"

Andy frowned, confused. Since when did Conner need a baby-sitter? And if his mom was in the market for one, he wasn't sure why she'd trust someone as famously irresponsible as Andy. Something serious was definitely up.

"Um, I guess so," Andy said lamely, fidgeting with the bottom of his Mean People Suck T-shirt.

"Good, good," Mrs. Sandborn said, nodding. "Okay, well, it was good to see you, Andy," she added, grabbing her keys from the hall table.

"Yeah, you too," Andy said, debating whether he should mention the state of her complexion if she was about to venture out in public. Deciding against it, he went ahead and walked upstairs.

Conner's door was closed as usual, and Andy could hear Santana playing from inside.

"Hey, McD," Andy called out, knocking twice. Conner pulled open the door, then immediately turned his back on Andy and walked over to his bed, flopping across it on his stomach. Andy noticed that Conner was wearing a long-sleeved navy shirt, even though it was pretty warm in his room. Conner wasn't exactly the type to dress up either.

I'm not here to question the guy's fashion choices, Andy reminded himself as he sat down on the edge of the bed.

"Okay, grouchy boy," Andy said. "What's with the bad mood? That fight with Liz last night?" He pushed aside Conner's blue comforter to make more room for himself on the sheets underneath. "Something with your mom?"

Conner groaned and dug his face deeper into his bed.

"Oookay, so Liz and your mom aren't good topics today," Andy said, circling his thumbs around each other. *Oh, no,* he realized. *I'm actually twiddling my thumbs.* Andy quickly separated his hands and pressed them down on either side of him on the mattress. "Actually, I came over here to talk about something else anyway."

"I'm fine," Conner grumbled.

Andy let out a short laugh. So now even Conner thought his friends' lives revolved around him? This was getting ridiculous.

"That's great, how you're fine," Andy said. He stood and started pacing around the room, noticing a bottle of vodka peeking out of one of the shelves on Conner's desk. How could Conner keep that lying around with his mom just back from rehab? Maybe she'd seen the vodka, and that's why she was so upset before. Andy flashed back to the state Conner had been in last night, when he left The Shack. Tia had mentioned something about worrying about Conner drinking a lot lately too.

What if she's right? Andy wondered. But even if Conner was in trouble, Andy still had to get this off his chest. He had to talk to someone who'd actually *care* that he was gay before he totally lost his mind.

"Listen, there's something I've gotta tell you," Andy blurted out, sitting back down on the bed. "Conner?"

Conner pulled himself up to a sitting position, then faced Andy. Andy's head jerked back in surprise when he saw how terrible his friend looked. Worse than Mrs. Sandborn—his eyes were red, and his skin was pale and pasty. Andy could even see the blue veins in Conner's forehead, casting a weird purplish tint to his face. "Are you sure you're fine?" Andy couldn't help asking.

When Conner's green eyes narrowed into a glare, Andy recognized the clear warning to leave it alone. If Conner didn't want to get into it, that was fine— for now. He could take his time with his problems. Just like Andy had taken time to deliver *his* news.

"So what is it you wanted to say?" Conner asked, scratching his head.

"Um, well . . . I'm sort of—I'm gay," Andy stated. He looked away, staring at the poster on the wall above Conner's bed.

Conner started to chuckle, and Andy felt his face heat up. Of all the reactions he'd imagined, laughter wasn't one of them.

"Wha-What's funny?" Andy stammered.

"Come on, Andy, you expect me to be surprised?" Conner asked. He tossed a pillow at Andy, who reached up to block it from his face.

"Wait—did Tia tell you?" Andy asked. "Or Liz?"

Conner scoffed. "No, they're too busy making sure I'm being a good little boy," he mocked.

The song that had been playing when Andy walked in the room ended, and as soon as the next one came on, Conner jumped up and went to raise the volume on his stereo. "This is a great song," he muttered, nodding his head to the music.

Andy frowned. He knew he should be relieved that Conner was taking this so well, just like the rest of Andy's friends had. But why wasn't *anyone* confused or *interested* to find out that he was gay? He certainly wasn't processing this too easily, and he understood what was in his own head better than anyone else.

"So why didn't you ever say anything?" Andy asked, swiveling his legs around the other side of the bed to face Conner as he moved across the room. "If you knew all along or suspected or whatever. Why didn't you ever tell me, like when I was going out with Six?" That had been horrible—trying so hard to be attracted to the cute, pretty girl he was dating but finding himself wanting to be closer to her *brother* than to her.

Conner shrugged, seemingly lost in the song as he mouthed along to the words.

Andy sighed. He reached down to flick a piece of fuzz off his khaki pants, kicking at the carpet with his shoe. This was pointless. Andy wanted to talk about this with someone, and he'd figured Conner

would be good because he wouldn't be so busy babbling about his life that Andy could fit a few words
in. But he hadn't counted on Conner being *so* quiet
that Andy felt like an idiot sitting there going on and
on about his sexual identity. The guy just didn't
seem to care.

"Okay, I'm gonna get going," Andy said as he
stood up. "I just wanted to let you know, I guess, and
you already did—so, hey, no point in sticking
around, right?"

No point if Conner didn't want to ask Andy if he
was going to tell his parents, if he was going to start
dating . . . or one of a million other questions that
Andy wished someone would ask him so that he'd
have to try to find answers.

Conner barely acknowledged Andy's words. He
was still standing next to the stereo, in deep concentration as the big guitar riff came to a climax.

"See you later," Andy mumbled as he left the
room. He stood in the hallway a second, wondering
if Conner would come after him. But he didn't.

*Maybe he's just really upset over whatever's bugging
him and his mom,* Andy thought as he walked down
the stairs. But it didn't matter anymore. Everyone
around him was always going through some new
"trauma." That didn't mean they couldn't take five
minutes off to care that Andy Marsden existed.

Andy ran a hand through the mop of red curls
on his head, glancing up the stairs one last time

before leaving. Everyone was always telling Andy what a great listener he was, how cool it was to know he'd be there for them all the time. Once Tia had joked that if Andy was ever the one in trouble, he'd need to clone himself to get good advice and support. Unfortunately, it looked like she was right.

Maria Slater

Is it really, really terrible if a tiny part of me is happy that Ken isn't the star quarterback anymore? I know this stuff with his dad is hard, and I know he misses playing. But when I look at the other guys on the team—jerks like Will Simmons or Josh Radinsky—I just can't help being relieved that Ken's not one of them. It's like their whole lives are just playing ball and hooking up with cute cheerleaders. I mean, I know Ken would never be like that anyway. But I guess it helps a little to know there's no chance it'll happen.

Jessica Wakefield

To: jaames@cal.rr.com
From: jess1@cal.rr.com
re: Big news

Jeremy,

   I have some <u>really</u> major news, but
I want to tell you in person. Come to
the game tonight at SVH, and we can
talk at halftime.

                         Jess

Beautiful Oblivion

Conner returned home from the beach, feeling better than he had all day—though not exactly *good*. After Andy had taken off, following his hilarious little "confession," Conner had decided to take a quick trip to Crescent Beach to clear his thoughts. His head still throbbed, and his stomach churned with some remaining queasiness, but the fresh salt air had stung the worst of it out of him. All he wanted to do now was play music.

For once fate had done him a favor because his mom and Megan still weren't back when he got home.

He was alone. *Finally.*

Closing his bedroom door behind him, Conner picked up his guitar. The familiar weight and shape of it offered a unique comfort. He grabbed a pick from the top of his dresser, then positioned the fingers of his left hand on the frets, gently pressing his fingertips down.

The pain seared, ripping through his open cuts.

Conner grimaced, then tossed the guitar roughly

down on his bed. He wouldn't be able to strum until his hands healed. And from the looks of them, that would be a week at least. The realization stung worse than the scrapes themselves.

Slowly he followed the path of cause and effect backward through his brain. He'd been drunk at the beach, and then he'd taken the fall. The fall caused the cuts. And the cuts were why he couldn't play. So drinking . . .

He shook his head, trying to reassemble the pieces of his thoughts. That was wrong—drinking hadn't caused this problem. He was missing a step, the one that came before the drinking. He'd left out all the crap in his life, the secrets, the hassles, the confusion. That stuff made him lean too far off that cliff last night because he had to find a way to stay out of reach of all the people in his life who never stopped needing *more* from him.

Elizabeth didn't understand. She thought he had a *problem* because he had a few drinks. What he had to get rid of wasn't the alcohol—it was everything else. Every*one* else. They'd even messed up his music now.

Conner flopped back on his bed, lying there facing the stucco ceiling. The phone rang as if on cue, and he ignored it, waiting for the answering machine to pick up. One ring. Two rings. Three rings. Then his message, abrupt and brief.

Beep.

"Conner? It's Liz. Are you there?" She paused. "Please call me. Please. I—I need to talk to you. Please, Conner."

Could the girl say *please* one more time? Conner pressed his eyes shut. He could hear her tears, just beneath the surface of the words.

"So, um, I'm going to the game tonight," she continued. "I don't know, maybe you'll feel like coming. Maybe I'll—maybe I'll see you there." It was like she wasn't even talking to him, but to herself. Trying to reassure herself that things were normal.

"Okay, well . . . I love you," she finished, her voice trembling.

Conner clenched his fists, resisting the urge to grab the phone. Elizabeth's pain ate into him—it was more excruciating than his aching hands and arms. But he couldn't let himself break down and talk to her. That would only get him tangled back up in what everyone else wanted him to be.

Conner stared hard at the phone as he heard the final *click* of Elizabeth hanging up. A mixture of relief and disappointment surged through him, and he instantly reached under his bed for the half-full bottle of Jack Daniels he'd stashed there the other day.

Conner raised the bottle to his lips. One drink was all he needed. Not even a drink—just a sip. Enough to smooth the edges, relieve the stress.

The rust-colored liquid was bitter on his tongue,

hot in his throat. It promised a burning, beautiful oblivion.

Ken shoved open the door to the guys' locker room and walked in, immediately surrounded by the sounds of his teammates getting changed and pumping each other up for the game.

Keeping his head bent down to avoid conversation, Ken trudged back to his locker and sank down on the bench in front of it, pulling off his shoes. He yanked open the lock and grabbed his uniform, shaking his head as he caught sight of the big red number on the back of his white jersey: 29. Ken remembered when the SVH cheerleaders used to paint signs with that number, chanting his name during games as he threw game-winning passes.

Now it felt pointless to even put the damn thing on, Ken thought. He'd be lucky to see even a couple of minutes of playing time, nothing that would give him a chance to really work his arm.

"Hey, Matthews," Aaron Dallas said, slapping Ken on the back. "What's wrong? You look spaced out."

Ken sighed. "I'm fine," he grunted in reply. Aaron gave him a strange look, then shrugged and walked to his locker a few feet away.

Aaron was a decent guy, and Ken didn't mean to sound like a jerk. But he'd never felt as frustrated with his position of warming the bench as he did today.

I guess I can thank my dad for that, Ken thought, remembering how his father would be out there in the stands, taking notes on Will's performance for his *Tribune* article. His dad's words this morning had stayed under his skin all day, and the scary part was that Ken was beginning to believe that maybe his dad hadn't been so off base. Maybe Ken really *was* a loser. Yeah, he had average grades now—better than he used to get, definitely. But he wasn't some genius like Maria. His talent was sports, and he didn't have that anymore. So what was left?

Ken took a deep breath, then finished getting changed, tying the laces of his cleats into a double knot. He stood up, swinging his metal locker door shut with a loud clang, then surveyed the other players in the locker room. His eyes landed on Will Simmons, who was already dressed. Will was hanging out near Josh Radinsky's locker, talking to Josh and Matt Wells. Ken flashed back to that scene in front of Chez Lorraine earlier. Will had to be on a serious thrill ride right now. Everything was falling into place for him.

Just then the door to the locker room swung open and Coach Riley came in, instantly silencing all the players. Ken respected his coach, even if he thought the guy had come down way too hard on him this fall. Coach Riley was smart and tough, and he kept their team at the top of the local ranks.

"It's almost time to get out there and start the warm-ups," Coach Riley instructed in his deep, commanding tone. He cleared his throat, placing his clipboard down on top of the locker next to where he stood. "Don't forget—a big part of winning is keeping the other team intimidated. So make sure you let them know the second you're on the field that you guys are *mean*." He paused, giving them a crooked smile. "Let's just run through today's plays one more time, then I want to see you out there kicking some Ridgefield butt. Got it?"

Ken's teammates roared their agreement, and Ken put in a weak growl of his own.

"Matthews—something wrong?" the coach called out, as if he had some kind of special hearing device to help him detect the slightest drop of enthusiasm in one of his players.

Ken licked his lips nervously. "My throat's a little dry," he said lamely.

"Well, get some water," Coach Riley replied. He launched into his brief summary of their plays, which Ken tuned out, figuring it wasn't anything he needed to know anyway.

Still, he did feel kind of bad about looking like he didn't have any spirit. He cared about the team, even if he wasn't a big part of it now.

I've got to get rid of this bad attitude, Ken decided, staring down at his shoes and shaking his head. *No matter how much it stinks that I can't play, once we're out on that field, I'm going to make sure I show these guys they have my support.*

Maybe Ken wasn't a star quarterback anymore, but he was still a team player.

Will arranged the fingers of his right hand on the laces of the ball, marveling at the perfection of the fit. It was as though his hand had been created for exactly this purpose—to throw a football long, far, and fast. He bent back his arm, then heard the *swoosh* of speed in his ear as he released the ball, sending it spiraling through the air. Will grinned as the ball landed precisely where he'd aimed it: In the safe crook of Todd Wilkins's arm.

So far, warm-ups were going great today. He had nailed every pass. His arm felt loose and strong, and there wasn't even a twinge in his knee from his fall earlier. He was on top of his form, and he knew it— he *felt* it in his entire body. Good thing too. His parents were making one of their rare appearances at the game, and Hank Krubowski was in the stands. Will didn't want the scout to have even a moment's regret about signing him.

Coach Riley called all the players to the bench, and Will jogged over, removing his helmet along with the other members of the team as the school band started to play the national anthem.

Will glanced over at the Ridgefield High players, decked out in their purple-and-gold uniforms. He scrutinized each of them, wondering who his toughest opponents would be.

"You can take those guys," a voice next to Will said. Will turned and saw Ken Matthews. Will and Ken weren't exactly best friends since they'd been competing for the same position back when the season started. At first Will had thought Coach Riley was seriously messed up for letting Ken rejoin the team after he quit, but at least Will's role as captain and starting quarterback had never been challenged. And even though the SVH guys on the team had been okay with having Will—an El Carro transfer—as their leader, they seemed to like having Ken around. It helped team morale, which made them play better. Which made *Will* look better.

"Yeah, number thirty-four looks kind of scary, though," Will said.

Ken followed Will's gaze and laughed when he saw the huge, burly guy Will was talking about.

"Man, that guy can*not* still be in high school." Ken shook his head.

"That's Jason Altman," Matt put in from behind Ken. "He's the biggest linebacker in the county."

The band finished playing the anthem, and Coach Riley started gathering the team in a group huddle before the start of the game.

"His stats are amazing," Matt continued to Will as they moved in closer to the bench. "But you're too quick for him—don't worry."

112

Will tried to focus as Coach Riley gave them their pregame pep talk, but his heart was beating so fast, he kept losing track of the words or just having trouble getting their meanings to his brain. Something inside Will told him that this was going to be a huge night for him—the biggest game he'd ever played.

Instinctively Will let his eyes wander over to the cheerleaders, searching for Melissa. He grinned when he caught sight of her in the short red-and-white skirt that showed off her amazing legs. Then he noticed she was holding up a big banner that read, Will Simmons Is Dynamite.

At that moment Melissa looked his way, and when their eyes met, she flashed him a wide, gleaming smile that gave him all the confidence he needed. She blew him a kiss, and he turned back to the coach, ready to go out there and cream Ridgefield High.

"Okay, guys, let's win this one!" Coach Riley finished up. After some shouts and hand slaps Will and the other starters jogged out to the field and got into position. Sweet Valley High had won the coin toss a couple of minutes ago, and they'd chosen to be the receivers. Will, who doubled as the Gladiators' kick returner, took his place at the fifteen-yard line. Every muscle in his body was taut with anticipation as he prepared to catch the ball when it came toward him.

The Ridgefield placekicker raised his arm, brought it down, then ran forward and kicked the ball, sending it flying. Will's eyes never left the foot-ball. He sprinted in the direction he expected it to land, snatching it out of the air just in time at the ten-yard line, and then took off toward the other end of the field.

Will could hear the wind through his helmet, along with the pounding footsteps of the Ridgefield defense players chasing after him. But somehow his legs kept bringing him farther and farther, and he faked out everyone who tried to block his path.

A part of Will registered when he passed the fifty-yard line, and his excitement sent even more adrenaline through him, pushing him to zoom faster down the field. He was almost at the other team's forty-yard line when two guys came at him from ei-ther side. He avoided one of them, and out of the corner of his eye he saw Matt try to take down the other guy. Will winced when Matt's efforts failed, still pushing himself forward, trying to get around the defenseman's trajectory. But right as he crossed the forty-yard line, the linebacker knocked into him, sending them both crashing down onto the ground.

When Will stood up, shaking the dirt off him, he realized that the people in the stands were whooping and cheering. He'd gotten *fifty yards*.

Will tried not to let himself get carried away by the exhilaration of his achievement. If he'd made it this far, he had to get those six points for his team.

Will continued to psych himself up while his

team gathered for the huddle. He called the play, asking Aaron Dallas to go long for a pass, then they broke off and got into position.

The whistle blew to begin the down, and Will clutched the ball in his hand, backing up as he waited for Aaron to run his route to the end zone. Will dodged the Ridgefield tacklers, keeping the ball alive while Aaron made his way to a clear spot. Finally Aaron was right where he had to be, and Will brought back his arm, then released the ball.

He watched in awe as the football whooshed through the air. A clean, perfect pass that landed right in Aaron's arms.

The crowd was on their feet, going totally, completely wild. And then it sank in. Will had made a touchdown pass on the *first play!*

Yes. Total euphoria filled Will's whole body, and a slow, amazed smile spread across his face as his teammates hurtled toward him, hooting and throwing their fists in the air.

I was right about tonight, Will thought, the energy surging through him. He was on fire.

Melissa finished her individual cheer for Will with a back layout that gave the crowd's screams for Will even more energy. She turned to face the stands, shaking her red-and-white pom-poms in the air above her head, trying to get the volume to ultimate capacity. Their kicker had easily scored the extra point after the touchdown, so SVH was leading 7–0 after the second play of the game. Melissa knew exactly what Will was feeling right now, and she wanted this moment to be perfect for him. For *them*.

Cherie came rushing over to Melissa, her auburn ponytail bouncing as she ran. "That was so incredible," Cherie gushed, her eyes wide with amazement.

Melissa smiled, imagining living out this experience over and over at college, with the TV cameras rolling. Maybe she'd even be interviewed to let the public know about the private side of Michigan's football star. And every girl at Michigan would wish she could be in Melissa's place.

Melissa cast a quick glance at Jessica Wakefield, who was in her position at the other end of the squad's lineup, standing between Tia Ramirez and Annie Whitman. This had to be killing Jessica—Will's big victory and Melissa shining in his spotlight. Jessica had tried her best to get Will away from Melissa, but in the end he'd come back to Melissa. Like he always would. Why had she been letting herself doubt that earlier?

"I can't believe how *fast* he ran," Cherie continued, tightening her ponytail. "No wonder he got that scholarship to Michigan."

"Yeah, seriously," Renee Talbot agreed from the other side of Cherie. "He's amazing."

Melissa beamed as she heard similar comments from people sitting on the bleachers. Being the girlfriend of the starting quarterback had some *major* advantages.

"Don't forget," Melissa said, "this is just *high* school. When we get to Michigan, Will and I will really have everything we want." She said the last part loud enough so that Jessica could hear. Jessica was warming up for one of the upcoming routines, her attention seemingly focused on her moves. Still, Melissa had a feeling Jessica had heard her because she kept messing up one of the steps.

Not that she's usually that coordinated anyway, Melissa thought, shaking her head.

"Yeah, Liss, maybe you're right about this college thing," Cherie conceded. She brushed her palm against her forehead to wipe away the few beads of sweat that had collected during their intense cheers when Will was running down the field. "You probably will have a lot of fun at Michigan."

Melissa let her mouth curl into a small, triumphant grin. She walked back to the table where the cheerleaders kept their water bottles and picked up hers, taking a couple of sips to cool down.

Glancing back out at the field, Melissa watched Will get into position for the next play. She squinted, trying to get a clear view through the still bright rays of the setting sun. Melissa blinked as she realized that Will was staring right at her. She broadened her smile, lifting up her slender hand to wave, and he waved back. She couldn't see his expression clearly, but she could picture his return smile, and that was all she needed.

Melissa marched back to the squad, feeling more confident than ever. "They're about to start," she said, directing her comment to Tia, their captain. "Maybe we should do the cheer—*if* everyone's ready, I mean," she added with a smirk at Jessica.

Tia shrugged, smoothing down her SVH sweater. She glanced around at the rest of the squad. "Okay, let's get in formation," she instructed.

Melissa stepped forward, taking her place between Gina and Renee. She rolled back her shoulders as she mentally prepared for the routine. If Will was going to keep blowing away the other team on the field, then the least Melissa could do was keep the crowd revved up to cheer him on.

Conner McDermott

Reasons Not to Show Up at the Football Game

Football sucks.

Liz will be there.

Reasons to Show Up at the Football Game

Get away from the house and my mother.

Nothing else to do.

Liz will be there.

Megan Sandborn

I know my mom and Conner like to protect me. That's why they never tell me that something's wrong until it's <u>really</u> bad, like when Mom had to go to rehab. But how stupid do they think I am? I've heard them fighting the past couple of weeks, and as soon as Wendy and I got in the car with her tonight, it was obvious she'd been crying. Then I mentioned Conner's name, and she started babbling about the new store that just opened in the mall.

So I guess I'm just wondering when they'll finally decide to let me know what's wrong this time.

Jessica jumped when she heard the loud noise, then realized it was just the starter's gun going off to signal the end of the first half of the game.

Wow—I really spaced out, she thought. She'd just been following Tia's lead for the cheers, barely even watching the action on the field. Her gaze kept wandering over to the bleachers, searching for Jeremy. She hadn't seen him arrive yet unless he'd snuck in while she wasn't watching and taken a seat out of her line of vision.

She knew she should have been paying more attention to the game, but it was getting annoying having to go crazy every time Will did yet *another* awesome move out there and then having to listen to Melissa and her little friends squeal over how great he was.

And it's not *that I still want him,* Jessica thought. Finally she could say that and know in every inch of her that it was really true. Seeing Will and Melissa together didn't hurt her anymore. She honestly just found them disgusting—pathetic. But

Will was a reminder of her mistakes—mistakes that had cost her someone a million times better than him.

"Hey, Jess?"

She forced herself to focus on Tia, who was standing in front of her, her wide, dark eyes narrowed in concern. "You have been seriously distracted this whole game," Tia said. "What's up?" She cocked her head. "Is it Liz? Is she really wrecked from last night?"

Jessica cringed as a stab of guilt hit her. Actually, she'd barely talked to her sister today. They'd driven to the game together, and Jessica had tried to get Elizabeth to spill more about her fight with Conner, but Elizabeth had just said she didn't want to deal with it.

"Um, no, I think she's okay," Jessica said. She sat down on one of the nearby gray folding chairs and stretched her tan legs out in front of her. "Did you talk to Conner at all today?" she asked, shielding her eyes from the stadium lights with her right hand so she could look up at Tia.

Tia shook her head. "I figured he could use some space," she said, plopping down in the chair next to Jessica. "So what's your latest?"

Jessica sighed, casting a sidelong glance at Jade, who was over at the drinks table with Annie. "You don't want to know," she mumbled.

Tia followed Jessica's gaze. "Is there an update on the Jade-Jeremy drama?" she asked.

Jessica dropped her head into her hands, groaning. Slowly she lifted her face back up, scrunching her features together in embarrassment as she met Tia's eye. "Jeremy sort of caught Jade with Josh last night," she said.

Tia's eyes widened. "*And?*" she prompted, raising her eyebrows.

Jessica squirmed on her chair. "And I *helped* him catch her," she added reluctantly.

Tia laughed. "No wonder the girl was flashing you death glares," she said, crossing her legs and tugging down her short cheerleader's skirt.

Jessica didn't even *want* to think about the kind of glares she'd get from Jade once she had to fire her. Why couldn't Ally have just done it herself? Jessica shivered, even though there was barely a breeze.

"So I guess they're over," Tia continued.

Jessica nodded. "Yeah, totally," she said, reminding herself that at least she had that to be grateful for.

"So what about you? Was he mad?" Tia asked.

Jessica sucked in her breath. "Big time," she said, flinching at the recollection of the harsh statements Jeremy had hurled at her on the beach. "He totally blasted me. But he came by work today and said he was sorry." Jessica stopped, looking over at Jade again. She was pretty sure Jade was out of earshot, but she lowered her voice anyway, edging her chair closer to Tia's. "He also said he was going to quit so he wouldn't have to work with her anymore," she explained. "But after I told Ally what was going on and how Jade's been a complete slacker, she got pretty upset. She said I have to fire Jade, so hopefully Jeremy will come back. But even if he doesn't—she wants Jade out of there."

Tia's mouth fell open. "So let me get this straight," she said, fixing Jessica with one of her don't-give-me-any-bull stares. "In two days you've cost this girl a boyfriend *and* a job."

Jessica's cheeks flushed. The way Tia said it, Jessica sounded like a major bitch. But *Jade* was the one who'd cheated on Jeremy and skipped out on work. Fine, maybe Jeremy and Ally wouldn't have *known* that information without Jessica clueing them in, but since when was it Jessica's responsibility to watch Jade's back? To hide her secrets?

Jessica stood up, leaning over to tighten the knot on her shoelace. She wasn't going to let Tia turn this around on her. She hadn't done *anything* wrong.

"Jess, I'm not—," Tia began, jumping up next to her.

"Forget it," Jessica cut her off. She looked up at the stands again, wondering where Jeremy was. What if he hadn't gotten her message? Halftime would be over soon. *I can talk to him after the game,* Jessica decided.

It would be better anyway. They could talk *away* from Jade. *And he'll still get to see me in my cute cheerleader's outfit,* Jessica thought, glancing down at herself approvingly. It couldn't hurt to remind Jeremy that Jessica actually had a body underneath the loose-fitting clothes she usually wore to House of Java.

Jeremy's actions last night and this morning had really blindsided Jessica—she honestly hadn't realized that he liked Jade that much. But deep down she was still convinced that he'd get over Jade soon enough. And then *finally* Jessica could have the chance to prove to Jeremy who he really belonged with.

Her.

Conner slid his fingers into two of the diamonds of the chain-link fence surrounding the SVH football field and pressed his forehead against the cold metal.

The second half had just started, and Conner was trying to hear what was going on, but the announcer's voice sounded fuzzy.

Probably the bad PA system, he thought.

He squinted at the players on the field. They looked kind of blurry.

Cheap stadium lights.

But what about the fact that the earth seemed to be tilting under his feet, causing him to keep losing his balance?

He was a little buzzed, that was all. Well, maybe more than a little. Which was why he'd been hanging out near the gate for the last five minutes, trying to decide whether or not to chance going over to the bleachers. If Elizabeth saw him right now, it would just prove her right about this whole stupid drinking-problem thing, when really it was only that he hadn't eaten much today, so the drinks had affected him more than he realized they would.

Still, as much as he didn't want to deal with a lecture, Conner really wanted to be near Elizabeth right now. If he could just hold her hand and smell that amazing flowery scent in her hair, he was sure that everything would be fine somehow. God, it had taken him years to let himself feel that way about another person—to trust that someone other than *him* could affect his emotions that intensely.

"Conner? What are you doing here?"

Conner let go of the fence and whirled around, coming face-to-face with Evan. The quick motion made Conner dizzy, but he tried not to reveal it to his new watchdog.

"Hey," Conner said, the word coming out more like a cold breath from his lips. "Why do you care?" he growled. He smirked as he observed Evan's trademark faded cargo shorts and Birkenstock sandals, topped with an unbleached woven sweater. The guy was just so *earnest*.

Conner turned back around and started heading for the entrance to the field. He wasn't in the mood to deal with the "friend" who'd ratted him out to

Elizabeth. With every step Conner felt like he needed to grab onto something solid to keep upright, but miraculously he was able to keep moving forward without falling—though he had a feeling his body was lurching a little. Either that or the ground really *was* shifting.

Conner heard Evan's quick footsteps as he chased after him, then came around in front of Conner to block his path. Evan pushed his straggly dark hair out of his face and raised his chin defiantly, his blue eyes taking on the stubborn glint that Conner recognized from whenever Evan got really into some speech about one of his pet causes.

Conner felt the vein in his neck begin to pulse. "I'm going to watch the game," he said through clenched teeth.

Evan didn't flinch. "Okay. We can go in together, then," he said. "Next time they call a time-out."

Conner laughed, managing to see the amusement factor in this situation despite being seriously annoyed with Evan's self-righteous behavior. "Look, Boy Wonder, I get it," Conner mocked. "You don't want me to go into the game because I think you're drunk." He frowned, shaking his head in frustration. "I mean, *you* think *I'm* drunk."

"I *know* you're drunk," Evan muttered. "And yes, I'm trying to get you to sober up just a little before you go in there and make a fool of yourself."

"What are you, my personal bodyguard?" Conner spat out.

"No, Conner," Evan said firmly. "I'm your friend."

"Right," Conner said, tugging at his hair. "My friend. The one who used to know when to mind his own business?"

Evan's face clouded over, but he took a step closer to Conner, pushing up the sleeves of his shirt to reveal his strong swimmer's arms. *Is that supposed to be some kind of threat?* Conner wondered. Maybe Evan was an athlete, but Conner could take him apart if a fight was what Evan wanted.

Conner placed his hands on Evan's chest and shoved him back a few steps. "I'm going inside," he said. "Come if you want. I don't care. Just stay away from me, okay?"

Conner stared at Evan hard, waiting to see his reaction. Evan met his gaze head-on, then glanced at something behind Conner, and his expression instantly grew anxious.

"Good evening, boys."

Conner swallowed, a bolt of fear shooting through him at the sound of the deep, lightly taunting voice. He turned around and saw a cop standing there, peering at him and Evan with beady eyes from under his dark blue hat. He was stocky, with reddish hair and ruddy skin—something about his build reminded Conner of a bulldog.

Damn. Conner had forgotten to pop in a breath mint before coming over to SVH. He probably had vodka on his breath, and his arm was still a mess. He took a few steps backward, moving next to Evan. Hopefully the cop would leave them alone once he knew there wasn't any problem between them.

"Hi, there," Evan said, smiling. Obviously Evan had the same idea. "We're just here for the game." Evan threw his arm casually around Conner's shoulders, and Conner figured it was as much to prove that they were friends as to keep Conner from falling down.

"Nice night for a football game, isn't it?" the cop asked, shifting his weight from one foot to the other as he continued to stare intently at Conner. "You missed a lot of the game, though."

"Actually, my girlfriend left her sweater in the car," Evan said quickly. "We were on our way to get it for her."

A wave of nausea overcame Conner, leaving a bad taste in the back of his throat. Puking on the officer's nice shiny shoes would be the *perfect* way to end this day.

"Okay, then," the cop said, his mouth twitching slightly. "You boys go on ahead and get that sweater. We don't want your girlfriend to catch a cold."

"Thanks," Evan said. Keeping his arm loosely around Conner, Evan started strolling out toward the parking lot. Conner walked along next to him, resenting the knowledge that he *needed* Evan's support to walk straight.

Once they were out of the cop's sight, Conner

shrugged away from Evan. "Okay, you did your good deed," he said. "I'm outta here."

Conner stalked off, the frustration building inside him starting to nullify the effects of the alcohol in his system. He wasn't drunk anymore, but he'd lost his desire to see the game, to see Elizabeth, to be around *anyone*. All Conner wanted was to be alone.

"Wait—you are *not* driving like this," Evan called out.

Conner waved his hand in the air dismissively. "I'm *fine,*" he yelled over his shoulder. At least he would be. If he was the only person existing on the planet.

The second the whistle blew, ending Ridgefield's time-out, Will tossed aside the cup of neon green sports drink he'd been guzzling, then hustled back onto the field.

Will had followed up his awesome play in the first half with another touchdown pass and then— seconds before the end of the half—a touchdown himself. Now the second half was almost over, and Ridgefield was coming up from behind. But SVH still had a decent enough lead to win the game pretty easily at this point. Still, Will was determined not to let up—he was going for every yard, every point he could get.

"Keep up the energy, guys," Will told his teammates as he entered the huddle, accepting their high fives. "Okay, Josh, option left," he instructed, choosing

130

a play that would allow him several choices if things got dicey. He could feel the heat coming from the Ridgefield team—they weren't liking the way this game was going, and they were starting to get rougher in their tackles. "Ready?" Will clapped. "Break!"

Will's veins pumped with pure energy as he called out the commands, then started the play, breaking toward the left side of the field with Josh following in case he needed to be bailed out.

At first Will avoided the Ridgefield defense easily, gaining yard after yard without having to pitch the ball back to Josh. But his muscles were getting tired from pushing himself to the limit this whole game, and he knew he should pass soon. No one was clear up ahead, but Josh was still right there behind him, waiting for a signal.

I can go a little farther, though, Will told himself, spotting a hole up ahead between the clusters of Ridgefield players. He didn't want to let go of the ball—he *couldn't* somehow.

Will kept pounding the ground, frowning as he realized that the hole was closing up—with Jason Altman, the huge linebacker, closing in on him.

Will risked a quick glance behind him to make sure Josh was there, ready. He was, and Will was preparing to pass the ball back to him when suddenly something enormous slammed into him from the right. The force sent him stumbling over, and he winced as he felt the ball slip out of his hands.

Lost it, he thought as he lurched awkwardly toward the ground, too upset over his fumble to care that he was falling. Finally the realization hit him that he was going down wrong. He tried to break his fall, instinctively extending his arms and letting his knees go soft.

But not soft enough. His right knee hit first—like a sledgehammer, smashing into the earth. He heard the pop—the sound echoed through his head, louder than anything he'd ever heard.

And then he felt it—felt the break. His kneecap seemed to tear away from the joint. The pain shot up into his thigh and down through his hamstring. In seconds it was everywhere, in his whole body. He opened his eyes, but his vision was hazy from the total agony spreading through him. Still, he could make out the players rushing toward him, leaning over him. Will bit down hard to keep from crying out, shutting his eyes again.

"Will?" It was Matt's voice. "Will, can you hear me?"

Will let out a soft groan in reply. He didn't think speech would be possible right now.

"Can you get up?" Matt asked. "Are you okay?"

Will tried to get his brain to send the signals to his leg, attempting to lift it from under him. The moment he moved, blinding pain coursed through him like lightning.

"Don't touch him," Will heard someone call out. "Don't try to move him. Coming through, coming through."

Will struggled to get his eyes open again and saw a blur of paramedics pushing their way through Will's teammates. They reached him, and Will heard the snip of a pair of scissors, then a tearing sound as the medic ripped his football pants at the knee.

"Man, it's swelling up like crazy already," the medic told his partner. "Someone tell the kid's parents to meet us at the hospital. We've gotta get him out of here, now."

The words filtered through Will's barely conscious mind. A wave of nausea rolled over his gut as he realized that this was *serious*.

"Will, I'm here," Will heard from behind the paramedics. The voice was soothing and familiar. But the note of terror in it wasn't.

"Liss?" Will forced himself to whisper. The effort in getting out the single syllable was almost unbearable.

"I'm here," she reassured him. "I'm not leaving you, okay?"

The paramedics slowly lifted Will onto a stretcher. As gently as they moved him, his knee still felt like it was shattering, splintering into a million agonizing pieces.

Soon the stretcher was being pushed across the field, toward the waiting ambulance. Will felt the tears gathering in his eyes, pouring down his cheeks. He'd never experienced physical torture like this before.

They loaded Will into the ambulance, and Will felt a soft, small hand grip his. He blinked a couple of times, seeing Melissa's face hovering over his.

"I'm right here," Melissa told him. "Your parents will be with you soon, but I'm here now."

Melissa. It was the last concrete idea in his brain before thought surrendered and understanding ceased. His knee throbbed so violently that all that remained was the pain, along with overwhelming, all-encompassing fear.

Evan Plummer

When we were kids, Conner and I used to push each other on the swings over at Tia's house. I was always really scared of falling off, so I used to hold on to the chains so tightly, my palms would get blisters. But Conner was never afraid. For him, it was all about getting higher and higher, no matter how much it freaked me out and I told him to slow down.

Once we got older, we pretty much stopped swinging and mostly just sat on the swings and talked about stuff, like his crush on the high-school girl who made the drinks at 7-Eleven and how he used to go there about thirty times a week just to have an excuse to talk to her.

Suddenly, though, I'm scared again—scared of him falling, but not off some dumb swing.

CHAPTER

Pure Instinct

9

Melissa sat perfectly still as the ambulance bounced over the field, then through the parking lot and out of SVH. The siren began shrieking as they sped toward Fowler Memorial Hospital. Will had lost consciousness a few moments ago, and the paramedic riding in the back with Melissa had explained that Will had probably passed out from the pain, and she shouldn't worry about it. At least Will wouldn't be in agony anymore.

Melissa reached over and brushed the sweat-dampened hair off Will's forehead. She squeezed her eyes shut and tried to pray over the screaming in her head. *Please let Will be okay.*

Opening her eyes, Melissa glanced around her at the inside of the ambulance, taking in all the medical equipment that surrounded her, objects she'd never seen before. Tim, the paramedic, sat across from her, on the other side of Will. He was monitoring Will's vital signs on some kind of machine. Tim looked pretty young, probably not too much older than they were.

This is some kind of movie or TV show, Melissa thought. *This isn't real.* But the noise of the siren and the scent of the medicines and the sight of the sterilized tools were all too vivid to be imagined. And Will lying there on the stretcher in front of her . . .

Melissa's chest constricted, and tears filled her clear blue eyes. She couldn't comprehend how any of this could be happening when just minutes ago, she and Will had been so close to total perfection.

"So—do you know what he did to himself?" Melissa asked Tim, her voice wavering. "I mean, what's wrong with his leg?"

Tim glanced up at Melissa, his brown eyes guarded. "We won't be able to tell until the doctor sees him," he replied. Melissa caught him gazing down at Will's right leg with a frown. She wanted to know how bad it was, but she couldn't bring herself to look. She'd gotten a glimpse of Will's knee back there on the field—long enough to see the blood and bone exposed.

"Just keep talking to him," Tim said in a low voice. "He's out, but he might be able to hear. We want to keep his pressure down, so it'll be good if you can help him stay calm."

Melissa gulped. "It's going to be okay, Will," she said, leaning back over him again. "I promise." Her voice caught in her throat as she worried that she was lying to him. She didn't know if he'd be okay—she had no *idea* what was going to happen.

Looking back at Tim, Melissa cleared her throat, anxious for reassurances even though it was obvious Tim wasn't handing out any. "He didn't hit his head, though, right?" she asked.

"There doesn't appear to be any head injury," Tim answered, reaching over to check something on Will's leg.

Melissa shut her eyes. If she got another look at Will's leg, she'd really fall apart. Will had held her together all these years, all the times when she'd been sure that if it wasn't for him, she would have just broken into a million pieces. Now it was her turn to prove that she could do the same for him.

"So it's—it's just his leg, then," Melissa said, her voice catching on the word *just*. She knew what Will's legs meant to him—what playing football meant to him.

Tim gave a brief nod. "I really don't want to say anything until the doctor examines him," he added. "But it does appear that the injured area is restricted to his leg. The spine seems okay."

Melissa let out her breath. She hadn't even thought about a spinal injury—the possibility of Will being paralyzed. But Melissa still knew that— for Will—a permanently damaged leg would be just as bad.

Biting her lip, Melissa returned her attention to Will. She brushed her hand over his cheek. "You're going to be fine," she murmured into his ear.

Maybe she was wrong, but as long as Will believed her enough to keep holding on, that was the best she could do.

Ken knew he should be feeling something right now. He'd seen the Ridgefield player, Jason Altman, steaming toward Will. He'd watched the guy slam into Will and then stared in shock as Will was knocked to the ground, his limbs coming down at all the wrong angles. Ken hadn't missed a second of the whole, disgusting scene.

But somehow nothing was really . . . *penetrating*. Ken was dimly aware of the way his heart had skipped in anticipation that first moment he saw Will go down. He'd thought maybe he'd have a chance to go in for a couple of plays if Will needed to rest for a few minutes.

But within seconds he'd realized that Will was hurt—bad. Then there were the paramedics, the ambulance, all of it happening around Ken while he watched, dazed and overwhelmed.

There were a million emotions Ken should be feeling—and guilt over his selfish impulse should be at the top of the list, right along with concern for Will.

But all Ken felt was numb. None of this made any sense to him. He kept flashing back to what he'd said to Jessica and Maria this morning, his offhand comment about taking Will down so that he'd be able to play. Ken didn't believe in fate, in making things happen just because you wished for them. So that couldn't be what happened here, right?

Ken gazed around at the rest of his team. Josh was pacing the sidelines, rubbing his forehead. Matt was sitting on the bench with his head in his hands. The other players were talking to each other in hushed tones, shaking their heads, or just sitting there, looking as stunned as Ken felt.

Coach Riley was having an intense conference with Ridgefield High's coach, along with the referees. After about a minute they broke apart, and the coach came back over to Ken and his teammates.

"We're finishing the game," he said. "We're all hoping Will's okay, but the best thing we can do for him now is bring this home, after all his hard work." He paused. "Matthews!" he barked.

Ken glanced up, feeling a strange twisting in his stomach. "Yeah, Coach?" he said.

"We need you in," the coach said, adjusting his ratty baseball cap.

Finally emotions surged through Ken at an overpowering rate, as if to compensate for the past few minutes of numbness. The guilt was there, definitely, but it was accompanied by so many other conflicting feelings that he could barely concentrate on any one thought.

"Let's go, Ken," the coach said. "Hustle!"

Ken grabbed his helmet from next to him and

put it on, snapping the chin strap in place. He sprinted out onto the field and joined his teammates in the huddle. Ken barked out a play, and the Gladiators broke into formation.

"Red, thirty-three. Red, thirty-three. Set. Hut. Hut!"

Brian Cogley, SVH's center, snapped the ball. Ken clamped his hand around it and dropped back into the pocket. He spotted Matt downfield—open. Wide open.

Ken gathered himself and brought back his arm, preparing to go long. But without warning, his grip buckled, and the ball wobbled out of his hand, landing in the grass a good fifteen feet away from Matt.

Nice going, Ken chided himself. A ten-year-old kid could throw better than that. At least it was still the Gladiators' ball.

Immediately the Ridgefield fans howled, mocking Ken. Ken looked around at his teammates, recognizing the disgust in their expressions. He could imagine what they were all thinking, how much they wished it was Will out here instead of Ken, the quitter who couldn't even throw a complete pass anymore.

Ken's head pounded inside his helmet, and the five cups of sports drink he'd chugged on the bench threatened to come up.

"What the hell was that?" Brian snarled.

"Huddle up, Cogley!" Ken ordered, cringing.

The rest of the players trudged toward him, the disgust in their faces giving way to pity. Ken almost preferred the disgust. He cleared his throat and massaged his throwing hand, trying not to remember that his dad was out there in the stands, probably more embarrassed about him than ever.

The team huddled up, waiting for Ken to call the next play.

"Wilkins, go wide," Ken commanded, keeping his voice firm and confident.

"Think you can reach him?" Josh spat, glaring at Ken from under his helmet.

Ken kept his eyes on Todd. "Break," he said curtly.

Ken took his place behind Brian. *Focus,* he told himself. *You're a good quarterback. You can do this. Just focus.* Then his voice echoed across the field: "Blue, fifty-two. Blue, fifty-two. Hut. Hike."

The snap was clean, and Ken backpedaled three graceful steps, angling his body in the direction he was going to throw. Todd busted through the pack of Ridgefield players, and Ken fixed his gaze on the receiver. Reading the defense, Ken broke to his right. Suddenly the game slowed down, and Ken was moving on pure instinct. The pocket was collapsing around him, and Ken scrambled away from several Ridgefield defenders. The crowd was going wild as the seconds ticked off the clock . . . but Ken didn't hear a word.

Todd was a moving target, his arms and legs

pumping ferociously. A trickle of sweat slid down Ken's forehead and stung his eye.

Ken heard a growl rumble in his own throat; panic turned his heart cold as he searched the far end of the field for Wilkins.

A second passed, then two, three ... and there he was.

Ken drew back his arm and released a perfect spiral.

Just as he threw the ball, a Ridgefield linebacker hit Ken from behind. His whole body shook from the force of the blow, and he hit the turf hard. Silence. Buried under the defender, Ken heard a thunderous roar as the ball was caught by Wilkins, who dove into the end zone.

Touchdown!

The fans on the bleachers went totally wild, and Ken realized that they were chanting *his* name. How long had it been since he'd heard that sound—the noise of a hundred people cheering for him? A year ago it was normal, ordinary. Now it was a high like he'd never dreamed of.

The player on top of Ken pulled himself off him, and Ken slowly stood, stretching out his arms. He turned to look at the stands, not fully believing what he'd heard from the ground. But the cheerleaders were singing his name, jumping, and clapping, and everyone else was still shouting for him.

Ken Matthews, star quarterback. Until this moment Ken hadn't had a clue how much that old title meant to him.

The buzzer sounded, officially ending the game, with SVH as the easy victors. Ken yanked off his helmet and started walking back toward the bleachers. Todd, still clutching the ball, jogged up beside Ken and gave him a hearty pat on the back.

"That was a great pass, man," Todd said, his brown eyes bright with excitement.

"Not a bad way to end a game, huh?" Ken joked.

Todd laughed, smacking his palm against the ball. "See ya in the locker room," he said, running ahead.

Ken continued at his even pace, relishing the feel of the soft grass giving beneath his cleats.

When he reached the edge of the field, his breath caught when he saw a familiar figure approaching him, beaming at him with a smile Ken hadn't seen in a long time.

His father. Somehow he'd forgotten him in the excitement of his touchdown play. Ken felt his heart jump almost instinctively at the sight of his dad, *proud* for once. But right away a cold flash of anger replaced the happiness. Sure, his dad was smiling at him—now that he had done something to *deserve* the smile. Ken's dad hadn't even shown up when Ken was awarded the Spirit Award at the county's athlete dinner, something plenty of parents would have been proud of.

The bottom line was that Ken's dad should have been there all along—even when Ken was bumped down to second string. A bitter taste flooded Ken's mouth. How dare his father grin like that, like it would cancel out everything else that had happened between them?

Ken's mouth set in an angry line, and he let his gaze lock onto his father's, staring back at him with zero emotion.

And then he turned his back and stalked away in the other direction.

Maria watched as Mr. Matthews stopped abruptly, his back stiffening. She'd been following him on her way to congratulate Ken, hoping that her presence would prevent any kind of major confrontation.

Maria hadn't been able to see the expression on Ken's dad's face, but she'd gotten a good look at the cold glare Ken had sent *him*. And she couldn't be happier that Mr. Matthews was finally getting what he deserved for treating his son so badly.

Slowly Mr. Matthews turned around, sinking onto the bleachers as the fans stepped around him to continue climbing down.

Maria still couldn't believe the events of the last fifteen minutes were real. Will Simmons being taken to the hospital, Ken finally getting to make his big play . . .

She sighed, tugging her thin jacket more tightly around her as a breeze swept by. Still staring at Ken's dad, Maria almost felt a twinge of pity at the confusion and hurt all over his features. But all she had to do was remind herself of how miserable the man had made Ken, and instantly all traces of sympathy vanished.

Mr. Matthews finally noticed Maria standing there, and she flushed as he frowned at her, narrowing his eyes.

Maria came down the few bleachers that separated them and sat down next to him. "So, Ken was pretty great out there," she said, pulling her long, flowered skirt under her legs to keep the wind from blowing it out around her.

"Yes," Mr. Matthews replied, his wide jaw tightening. "That's my boy."

Maria held back a bitter laugh. "Actually, Will's the player you usually write about, isn't he?" she asked innocently. "But Ken's pass looked just as good as the one Will Simmons threw in the beginning of the game, don't you think?"

Mr. Matthews's frown deepened. "Ken could outthrow Will any day," he mumbled. "But he screwed up, lost his chance to play."

"So," Maria pressed, leaning toward Ken's dad. "The crowd really loves him, you know. But then again, some of us never gave up on him in the first place."

Mr. Matthews flinched. He clutched the notebook he was holding tighter in his hands, looking down at his lap.

"Fans can be fickle," he said, his facial muscles twitching. He paused, then glanced back up at Maria. "But you're right," he said. "The crowd really did love that play. Especially the cheerleaders. Girls love a football hero, you know." He smiled. "But you're not really a big sports fan, right?"

Maria sucked in her breath, breaking from his gaze. She fiddled with the zipper on her jacket, pulling it up and down.

Ken's dad was a jerk—but what if he was right? She knew it was crazy to take his comment seriously. Still, it seemed like Will was hurt pretty badly, which meant that tonight had probably been only the first game for Ken. Maria had no idea if it would change things between them for Ken to get back into his old life, the one that *she* hadn't been a part of.

"So, I guess I'll be fielding a lot of calls for the kid now," Mr. Matthews said as he stood and buttoned up his brown jacket. He clapped his notebook shut. "I'll see you later, Maria," he said, starting off down the steps.

Maria glanced around at her at the emptying bleachers. Almost everyone had left except a few stragglers. She saw a couple of sophomore girls still gathering their stuff at the other end, chattering a million miles a minute about something. Maria wondered idly if they were babbling about the new hot quarterback.

Don't let him get to you, Maria told herself,

smoothing down her skirt as she stood up. Mr. Matthews was just angry that after rejecting his son for months, he wasn't welcomed back with open arms once Ken was suddenly the big football hero he'd always wished for. The man didn't know anything about Maria and Ken's relationship.

But Maria did—she knew that they were solid. So why was she suddenly so worried?

HANK KRUBOWSKI'S AFTER-GAME NOTES

- Simmons out with knee injury, looks pretty serious. Might not be able to play. Check condition with hospital in a few days.

- Matthews back, talented junior we scouted last year. Still has a great arm. Worth following up.

Never. Play. Again.

Jessica finished packing away her cheerleading uniform in her gym bag and zipped the bag shut, then closed her locker door. She still felt like she was moving in slow motion. Ever since she'd seen Will fall, then heard the growing panic around her as the medics ran out onto the field, it was taking her longer to process her thoughts.

Even if Jessica was over Will, seeing him so badly injured was still a serious shock. *It's not like you can watch a guy you used to date taken away in an ambulance and not feel* something, she thought.

"—lissa went in the ambulance with him," Gina was telling Cherie. They were standing on the other side of the girls' locker room, still getting changed back into their clothes. "We should call her later to see how Will's doing."

Jessica shook her head, feeling genuine sympathy for Will and Melissa despite how little respect she had left for the couple. Jessica couldn't imagine how scared Will was right now. Football was his life— what if he was out for the whole season?

"You almost ready to take off?"

Jessica glanced up, pushing her blond hair back behind her ears. Tia stood in front of her, wearing the maroon boat-neck shirt she'd had on before the game.

"Um, pretty much," Jessica answered. She considered running out to the field to do one last check for Jeremy but decided against it. She'd searched the bleachers twice before coming into the locker room, and Jeremy was nowhere in sight.

Why wasn't he here? Didn't he get her e-mail? It wasn't like him to just ignore her like that. Unless he was still messed up over the whole Jade thing.

Jessica glanced across the locker room at Jade, who was standing in front of the mirror over the sinks, carefully running a brush through her silky black hair. For a girl who'd just been dumped, Jade seemed perfectly fine. No sign of crying, and she hadn't messed up a single step of their routines out on the field.

The girl was just *cold.* That had to be it. Jessica couldn't even believe that they used to be friends. She'd been having some serious failures of judgment this year. At least if Jade kept acting like this, it wouldn't be as tough for Jessica to break the news to her about being fired.

"Okay, all ready," Jessica told Tia, who was shifting impatiently. Jessica stood up and hoisted her black canvas bag over her shoulder.

Maybe I could stop at Jeremy's on the way home, Jessica thought, glancing up at the digital clock above the lockers.

"Great," Tia said, heading toward the exit. "So should we go find Liz? I saw her in the stands before," Tia continued over her shoulder. "She looked pretty bad."

Jessica blinked. "Yeah, let's try to find her," she agreed, remembering that her sister's love life was in seriously critical condition. A relationship in trouble definitely ranked above a nonexisting one. *Nonexisting for now,* Jessica reminded herself. Hopefully not for much longer.

Elizabeth strolled through the crowds of students toward the parking lot, barely noticing as her shoulders continued to get shoved from all directions when she didn't move quickly enough.

Elizabeth was dimly aware of being surrounded by noise—cheers, shouts, and excited chatter from everyone as they made their way across the SVH property. But it was as if someone had pressed a mute button on all outside sounds, causing the noise to filter into her head to be fused together as one low, unintelligible hum.

Elizabeth had watched Will Simmons disappear in an ambulance. She'd seen Ken finally get the chance to achieve something that meant so much to him. Those were huge moments. But the only thought that had stuck with her this whole night was that Conner wasn't there.

He never showed up.

All the worries, the fears that had shrieked in her mind all day . . . they were quiet now. There was an eerie stillness in her. Not peace—anything but. Just a cold, aching *void*.

Elizabeth sighed, rubbing her palms against the sides of her black capri pants. Maybe she was just tired. Tired of thinking so hard and so *loud*.

"Liz! Liz—wait up."

Elizabeth stopped and turned around. Jessica and Tia were rushing toward her, waving. Tia was running faster since her movement wasn't impeded by her loose cargo pants. Jessica had on one of her tight khaki skirts, so she wasn't quite as fast.

Elizabeth swallowed, wishing she'd made it to the Jeep before her sister and Tia had caught her. Jessica could have gotten a ride, and Elizabeth wouldn't have had to face their sympathetic expressions and the questions she had no answers for.

"Hey," Tia panted, stopping to catch her breath when she reached Elizabeth. "Thought you might want some company," she said, pulling her dark brown hair into a knot at the back of her neck. "HOJ or the Riot?"

Elizabeth hesitated. The calm in House of Java would make her want to scream—but the crazy, packed dance floor at the Riot would be suffocating.

Besides, she couldn't imagine either place without seeing Conner in them—lounging back in one of HOJ's comfy chairs or leaning up against the bar at the Riot.

The bar. Drinking. Conner drinking. Elizabeth reached up to rub her temples.

"Or we could rent a movie," Jessica suggested. She'd jogged up to them just in time to catch Tia's last words. "Anything with John Cusack would work for me right now," she added, tilting her head.

Elizabeth glanced at her sister, meeting her gaze. She stared into the blue-green eyes that mirrored her own, hoping Jessica would be able to read her emotions.

"Or, you know, we could all just head home," Jessica said quickly, giving Elizabeth a faint smile. She turned to Tia, shifting her black bag higher on her shoulder. "It was a pretty intense game, and maybe we could use some time to, um . . . " She trailed off, shrugging helplessly. "Liz? What do you think?"

Tia frowned, fixing Elizabeth with an intent gaze. "I'm getting a real leave-me-alone vibe here," she said. "So I guess I'll take off. But give me a call to-morrow, okay?"

Elizabeth nodded. "Thanks, Tee," she said softly, grateful that her friend wasn't pushing. Conner was in trouble, and she'd have to spill everything to Tia soon—if Evan didn't take care of that for her. But she didn't have the energy for that particular drama right now. In fact, Elizabeth was starting to wonder if she had any energy left in her at all.

Will Simmons woke up early on Sunday morning to broad beams of sunshine streaming through his window.

He blinked, wanting to stretch, but his body was sore and his brain fuzzy. His haze-clouded eyes darted around the room.

TV up on a shelf, metal rails on the bed, curtain running the length of the room.

Will frowned. The elements were familiar if he could just place them. Wait—he was in a *hospital* room. Why?

Will closed his eyes again, trying to summon the information. That was when he heard the soft sniffling sound coming from the corner.

Melissa. Crying.

His mind spun backward in time. Melissa . . . hospital. She'd tried to kill herself. His fault for breaking up with her. Was he here to visit her again? Or still? What day was this? What month? Had he dreamed her recovery? Were they back where they started, or was this later—now—and she'd tried to do it again?

The anxiety flooded Will as he tried to make sense of where he was and why Melissa was crying.

The memory attacked him suddenly, as viciously as

the linebacker had. *Josh, option left. Oomph. Swelling up like crazy.*

This wasn't about Melissa. This was about *him*. Will groaned as the pain of the injury cut through his confusion—a throbbing, stabbing pain in his leg, an agony that radiated from his knee to every inch of his body.

"Liss?" he croaked, forcing his eyes back open.

"Will!" She was at his side instantly, grasping his hand in hers and focusing her beautiful blue eyes on his face. "I'm here, Will. Your parents just went to get some coffee, but they'll be back."

Will tried to swallow, but his throat was unbearably dry. "How bad is it?" he managed to get out.

Melissa hesitated, glancing down at their joined hands. "Guess what?" she said, her voice full of obviously fake enthusiasm. "The cheerleaders sent a balloon bouquet last night, but the nurses made your parents take it home. They said if one popped, the noise might give some patient a heart attack." She laughed, a hollow, strained sound that caused Will's heart to beat faster in fear.

"How bad?" he repeated, his voice getting stronger. He struggled to sit up but was overcome with a wave of wooziness that sent him crashing back down onto the pillow.

Melissa's grip on his hand tightened, and he could feel her long fingernails digging into his skin. His memory went back to brunch yesterday and the sound Melissa's nails had made against the glass she was lifting for Hank Krubowski's toast to him.

"They brought me the breakfast menu to fill out," Melissa rambled on. "I ordered you pancakes. And orange juice. I know you like grape juice better, but they didn't have it, so I—"

"Stop," he said firmly, gritting his teeth. "My knee. How bad is it?"

Melissa leaned over the bed, her eyes glistening with tears. She reached up with her free hand and brushed the hair back from his eyes. "You should really talk to the doctor," she said, her lips trembling. "I'm not—"

"Tell me," Will demanded, licking his lips.

Melissa glanced over at the doorway, then back at Will. She drew a deep breath, lowering her eyes so she didn't have to meet his gaze. "They had to do emergency surgery last night. Three hours. Your dad made sure you had the very best surgeon on the staff."

"And?" Will prompted, fighting back the intense stabbing sensation in his leg.

Melissa bit her lip. "They said you won't be able to play," she whispered.

Will closed his eyes, trying to keep himself steady. The Gladiators were having an amazing season. They were just a few games away from the play-offs, and playing in the championships was almost a sure thing—with him as the quarterback. But without him the team would be in trouble. And he would never get the chance to achieve a high-school championship victory.

"Will?" Melissa said, her voice soft, shaky. "Are you okay?"

Will forced his eyes back open. Sitting out the rest of the season would drive him crazy, but at least he still had Michigan. He'd train twice as hard to get back in shape for next fall, and playing in Division I would make him forget all about missing a couple of months of high-school ball. But right now he needed to reassure Melissa. Her face was so *pale*.

"Yeah, I'm okay," Will said, trying to smile. "Don't worry, I'll be fine by summer practice," he joked, coughing.

A strange, almost *scared* expression came over Melissa's features, and she pressed her lips together even tighter. "No, you don't—" She stopped, letting out a short breath. "Will, they don't think you'll *ever* play again."

Never. Play. Again.

Will felt the pain surge. Then he felt the warmth of Melissa's tears as she pressed her face to his.

And then he felt nothing.

JEREMY AAMES

SATURDAY, 11:34 P.M.

I wonder what Jessica wanted to tell me. Should I call her? No, it's too late. If only she hadn't said it was <u>really major.</u> This is going to drive me crazy. Man, I wish I'd checked my e-mail sooner. It's fine, Aames. I'll call her tomorrow. I'm sure it can wait until then.

I've gotta stop letting Jessica Wakefield get to me like this!

ELIZABETH WAKEFIELD

SUNDAY, 12:01 A.M.

When I was (trying desperately not to be) falling for Conner, I did a really good job of making Maria believe that I couldn't stand him. Tia saw right through me, maybe because she was used to watching girls throw themselves at her best friend. But it wasn't too hard to hide my real feelings from Maria, someone who knows me so well.

I guess it was because Conner's nothing like what Maria and everyone else thought my "type" was. I mean, Conner could definitely never be confused with Todd Wilkins. Conner is everything that's wrong for me. Except somehow he's everything that's right too. At least . . . he was.

I'm worried about Conner, about his drinking, but I'm also scared of something else—something that never seemed possible until now. I'm scared that maybe things have changed—that as much as I love Conner and want him to still be right for me, he might not be anymore.

KEN MATTHEWS

SUNDAY, 2:34 A.M.

Man. I forgot how tough it is to fall
asleep after the rush of a great play.

MARIA SLATER

I cannot believe I just dreamed that Ken turned into a giant football and got carried off the field by Melissa Fox. This is really insane.

Okay, so Ken didn't wait for me outside the locker room after the game like he normally does. But he _did_ leave a message on my machine, explaining that the guys on the team dragged him off to celebrate, and it's not like we had actual plans or anything. I even told him before that I wanted to be home early tonight to get some sleep.

Maria, you're a totally paranoid freak. You'll call him tomorrow morning, and everything will be fine.

So why can't I get my heartbeat to slow down enough to fall back asleep?